I need you to come to me . . .

Something was calling her name. Not out loud, but inside her, whispering in soft, oddly familiar tones, *Margaret, please come to me. Please, I need you to come to me!*

Margaret clung to her bed, riveted by terror. Though she couldn't say what was calling, she knew all too well where it was calling from.

The pond.

As she had always known would happen, something in those murky waters was calling to her, desperately, urgently summoning her to come to it.

"I won't go," she whispered. "I *won't* go!"

But still the voice called and called. . . .

BRUCE COVILLE'S BOOK OF

SPINE TINGLERS
TALES TO MAKE YOU SHIVER

Compiled and edited by
Bruce Coville

Illustrated by
John Pierard

A GLC Book

AN
APPLE
PAPERBACK

SCHOLASTIC INC.
New York Toronto London Auckland Sydney

ISBN 0-590-25930-X

Copyright © 1996 by General Licensing Company, Inc. All rights reserved. Published by Scholastic Inc. APPLE PAPERBACKS is a registered trademark of Scholastic Inc. Cover artwork copyright © 1996 by General Licensing Company, Inc.

"The Thing in Auntie Alma's Pond" and "Welcome to the Shiver Factory!" copyright © 1996 by Bruce Coville.

"Letters from Camp" copyright © 1981 by Al Sarrantonio.

"Vampire for Hire" copyright © 1996 by Patrick Bone.

"One Chance" first appeared in *Werewolves* edited by Jane Yolen and Martin H. Greenberg [Harper & Row, 1988]. Reprinted by permission of author. Copyright © 1988 by Charles de Lint.

"Grendel" copyright © 1996 by Mary Frances Zambreno.

"Jenny Nettles" copyright © 1996 by Debra Doyle and James D. Macdonald.

"Those Three Wishes" copyright © 1982 by Judith Gorog.

"What's a Little Fur Among Friends?" copyright © 1996 by Sherwood Smith.

"The Sight of the Basilisk" copyright © 1996 by Lois Tilton.

"The Teacher Who Could Hear" copyright © 1996 by Paula McConnell.

"Life With a Slob" copyright © 1996 by Gordon Van Gelder.

"Campfire" copyright © 1996 by S. Anthony Gardner.

"Past Sunset" copyright © 1996 by Vivian Vande Velde.

10 9 8 7 6 5 4 3 2 1   4 5 6 7 8 9/9 0/0

Printed in the U.S.A.   40

First Scholastic printing, January 1996

For Patty Parsons Reagan

CONTENTS

WELCOME TO THE
SHIVER FACTORY!

Come in, sit down, relax.

Have I got a story for you.

Thirteen stories, in fact—thirteen little bundles of fear to give you your daily dose of vitamin H (for horror).

Of course, these stories aren't going to stick to your ribs. They may, however, stick to your spine—or the inside of your skull. Something about fear tends to stay with a person.

Heck, I can still name the scariest story I ever read, even though it's been over thirty years since I saw it.

I was in, oh, fifth or sixth grade, and I got a book called *Stranger Than Science*—a collection of weird events the author claimed were thoroughly documented. One of the first stories in the book was a piece of nastiness called

Introduction

"Invisible Fangs"—a tale about a little girl who claimed she was being attacked by invisible vampires. She would come screaming into the town square, clawing at her neck and . . . No, I'd better not tell you the details. They scare me even now!

The strange thing is, they might not scare *you* at all. For example, when I loaned *Stranger Than Science* to my across-the-street neighbor, he was terrified all right—but by a completely different story!

I've been thinking about what that means, and I've decided that fear is a very personal matter. What scares the daylights out of one person might leave another completely cold. I suspect this has to do with the twists and turns of our own lives, the odd corners of our brains, the things that happen to us before we're even old enough to speak.

Whatever the reason, there are stories that are merely scary, and there are stories that reach inside and touch us in a place so deep that we can never completely shake them off.

That's not necessarily a bad thing. A story that hits you that strongly can probably tell you something important about yourself—if you can stand to think about it once you get done screaming.

Well, that's one reason we've got thirteen different stories here. After all, if the ghosts don't get to you, maybe the vampires will. And if it's not the vampires, then maybe it will be one of the werewolves, or the strange serpent lurking in an ancient tomb, or the dinosaurs, or one of the other horrors waiting in the pages that follow. I hope at least one of them will send that delicious shiver the French call a *frisson* shooting up your spine.

It happened to me. One of these stories literally made me shiver with horrified delight.

I'm not going to tell you which one, of course. After all, it may be a completely different tale that leaves *you* looking over your shoulder once the sun has set.

As I said, fear is very personal.

But let me point out something else. Even though "Invisible Fangs" terrified me so much I couldn't get to sleep without the lights on for several nights after I read it, *I didn't stop reading scary stuff.*

After all, there's something strangely pleasant about getting scared, don't you think?

So . . . welcome to the shiver factory. My fellow authors and I have been working overtime to make your spine tingle.

If we've done our job well and you find yourself lying in your bed in the middle of the night wondering if you're going to make it through till morning, just remember this: Unlike the book that scared me so much when I was a kid, these stories aren't true.

The authors made them all up.

At least, that's what they told me. . . .

We have a family friend who has a pond behind her home. One summer night when my daughter and I were out walking on a country road and passed a similar pond, she shivered and told me that our friend's pond was the scariest thing she knew. Which got me to thinking . . .

THE THING IN AUNTIE ALMA'S POND

Bruce Coville

Water.

Margaret hated water.

So why was she standing at the edge of Auntie Alma's pond, staring at the black water as if she could see more than a few inches past the murky surface?

As if she were looking for something.

A dragonfly flickered past her, the light on its wings startling her out of her thoughts.

She raised her eyes to look again at the little rowboat that floated in the middle of the pond. *Why is it anchored there?* she wondered uneasily. It seemed strange to see it caught between the banks like that, not free to drift to one side or the other.

Margaret shrugged. Probably one of her cousins had done it. They were always playing pranks like that.

Still, it would be nice if a few of the cousins were around now. Auntie Alma's place was too quiet without them. Margaret sighed. She wished the rowboat was back on the shore, where she could get at it. If the cousins were here, she might be able to talk one of them into swimming out to get it for her.

Margaret turned and started back toward the house. It would be a long time before she forgave her parents for leaving her here like this. The separation had been bad enough. Now, to "work on getting back together," they had shoved her off on Auntie Alma . . . left her here to rot for the summer while they tried to "find themselves," or some such thing.

Why didn't they try to find *her*, instead? She had been feeling lost for some time now. And being exiled from her home and friends like this was no help.

Margaret kicked savagely at a silver dandelion, setting its seeds free to float away on the summer breeze. If her parents did have to send her away for the summer, couldn't they have found someplace besides Auntie Alma's? Sure, it was out in the country, and the fresh air was probably good for her. But there was no one around to play with, no one to even talk to except Auntie Alma, who wasn't her real aunt anyway, for heaven's sake, just an old friend of the family.

A really old friend, if you wanted to get right down to it, thought Margaret unkindly. Indeed, white-haired Alma Jefferson was a truly ancient collection of crotchets and wrinkles. She had a huge, hairy mole on her chin that Margaret found simultaneously fascinating and repugnant. Her hearing was bad, her eyes were weak, and she put her teeth in a glass on the kitchen shelf every night. Margaret especially hated that. Something about the sight of those false parts soaking in their cold water always made her shiver.

Stop it, she told herself, as she went through the back door of the house. *You're being cruel.*

In fact, pausing to think about it, Margaret remembered how much she had loved Auntie Alma when she, Margaret, was younger—how when she was frightened, she would throw her arms around the old woman's waist and whisper, "I'm always safe with you."

That memory made it all the more painful when Margaret entered the kitchen and saw the slight look of disappointment that flickered across Auntie Alma's face.

Though the expression vanished almost instantly, it stabbed Margaret to the heart. *I guess she doesn't want me around either,* the girl thought bitterly. *Probably she was hoping I'd drown while I was out at the pond.*

Margaret shuddered at the thought, which she knew wasn't fair. The thing was, she had been afraid of Auntie Alma's pond for as long as she could remember—which wouldn't have been so bad, if not for the fact that everyone else in the family seemed to think it was the most wonderful place in the world.

How they had teased her for not wanting to go in, for drawing back from its murky waters. "For heaven's sake, Margaret, come on in and cool off," her mother would exclaim from the pond on those hot summer afternoons when they came here to escape the city. "You like the pool in town. What's wrong with this?"

But Margaret could never explain her fear of the pond, the sense of nameless dread that seized her whenever she stood on its grassy bank and imagined stepping down into the black water.

The feeling that something was *waiting* for her there.

That was why she had always preferred the boat. It held her safely above the pond, its wooden floor a comforting barrier between herself and the terrifying water.

Still, those fears had been only a small part of her life back in what she now thought of as "the good old days"—the time when Mom and Dad had been happy together, not acting as if being married was some miserable job they had been forced into. She sighed. Why did grownups have to make such a big deal out of everything, anyway?

She wished her friend Lisa Meltzer could have come here with her. Or, better yet, that she could have stayed at Lisa's house, where she always felt welcome and wanted. Too bad the Meltzers were away on vacation.

Auntie Alma made supper and set it on the table. "A summer supper," she said cheerfully, as she always did when she put out this kind of meal. It consisted entirely of fresh things from her garden—thick-sliced tomatoes, red as blood, each bite packed with more flavor than a dozen of the pale, hard things Margaret's mother bought at the grocery store in the winter; yellow squash, glistening with melted butter, seeds nearly clear from the steaming; and baby carrots, torn early from the ground.

The only thing not from the garden was dessert—Auntie Alma's special molasses cookies. Though Margaret had loved them since she was little, tonight she couldn't bring herself to touch them.

"Goodness, sweetheart," clucked the old woman, "you haven't eaten a thing."

Margaret stared at the soft, homely face quivering with concern. "I want to go home!" she shouted.

The look of worry and sorrow in Auntie Alma's eyes was too much to bear. Margaret bolted from the table and fled to her room.

For the next hour she lay on her bed, staring at the ceiling. She was being horrible and she knew it. Auntie Alma hadn't done anything wrong, had only been worried about her.

But she couldn't help herself. Nothing seemed right, and the knot of fear that had tied itself inside her left no room for food, not even Auntie Alma's cooking, which was, she had to admit, delicious.

But not now.

Not now.

After a long while, Margaret slept. She had a dream where a familiar voice was calling to her, calling her to come into the darkness. She woke with a gasp.

To her horror, the voice was still calling to her, not out loud, but inside her somehow, whispering in soft, oddly familiar tones, *Mar-*

garet, please come to me. Please, I need you to come to me!

She clung to her bed, riveted by terror. Though she couldn't say what was calling, she knew all too well where it was calling from.

The pond.

As she had always known it would some-day happen, something in those murky waters was calling to her, desperately, urgently, sum-moning her to come to it.

"I won't go," she whispered, tightening her-self against the bed as if she could actually press herself into the mattress, merge with it so that nothing could pull her away. "I *won't* go!"

The voice called and called, until finally Margaret shouted out in terror. Then Auntie Alma came and sat beside the bed and sang to her. The old woman's face was sad, and her wise old eyes seemed to hold some terrible se-cret. But her voice was comforting, and even better, her reassurances about bad dreams man-aged to drown out the voice that still called and called from the pond.

Finally Margaret slept.

When she woke, she noticed water on the floor. From the dank smell, she knew that it had come from the pond.

Late the next morning, somewhat to her astonishment, she found herself standing at the edge of the pond again. A surge of panic rippled through her. She didn't even remember walking here! She swallowed nervously. Was the call of whatever waited beneath the water so strong that it could draw her here against her will? How much longer could she resist if she could end up here without even realizing it?

She forced herself to back away from the water. After three steps, she turned and started to run up the ridge that separated the pond from Auntie Alma's house.

Halfway to the top she stopped, looked back.

The boat still floated in the center of the pond. The black water surrounding it was smooth and mirrorlike, for the hot air held no hint of a breeze.

Margaret looked past the boat to the far side of the pond. A row of willows grew at the edge, their thick old trunks standing so close to the water it looked as if they were about to go wading. Their drooping branches overhung the pond, shading it for much of the day. Fallen leaves, narrow and shaped like the tips of spears, dotted the surface of the water.

Beyond the willows the land sloped up to a forested area. It was dark and mysterious, yet somehow as inviting as the pond was terrifying.

Margaret remembered a summer day years

ago, when she was only three or four years old. She had been happily playing on the grassy bank at the edge of the pond when her father's brother, Uncle Ted, had reared up from the water, roaring and pretending to be a monster. Murky water streamed from his long hair, poured from his grasping fingers as he stalked forward, growling, "I'm going to get you, Margaret!"

She had shrieked and run for her mother. The grown-ups, all the aunts and uncles and cousins, had laughed. Only Auntie Alma had disapproved. Margaret still remembered with satisfaction the way that the old woman had bawled out Uncle Ted.

Many times since then Margaret had watched grown-ups play with children, and she was amazed at how often adults seemed to think it was a game to frighten little kids. Yet the kids often laughed at those times. When she saw that, she wondered if the kids really meant it, or if they were just trying to hide their fear. Was it possible that they actually did like it? Was she really that different from all the others?

Probably, she thought bitterly. She had always been different. She should be used to it by now.

With a start, she realized that Auntie Alma

was standing beside her. She hadn't heard the old woman approaching.

"Are you all right, dear?"

Margaret didn't answer right away. She wasn't all right, not really. But she didn't know that there was anything Auntie Alma could do to change that—except send her home, of course. Which didn't seem likely.

"I'm afraid," said Margaret at last.

The old woman nodded. "It's hard when things change," she said. "Gets a person all stirred up inside."

Margaret relaxed a little. Maybe Auntie Alma understood better than she thought. She waited a moment and then said, "I'm afraid of the pond."

Auntie Alma didn't answer for a while. When she did, her voice was soft and sounded faraway somehow. "No need to be afraid of it anymore," she said. "Not now."

"What does that mean?" asked Margaret.

The old woman laughed. "If I told you everything you wanted to know, it wouldn't leave anything for you to find out on your own."

"Good thing you're not a teacher," said Margaret teasingly.

"Oh, the very best teachers never tell you everything, my dear. The best teachers know that you have to figure some things out for yourself. After all, what's life without a little mystery?"

That night rain was pattering lightly against the window when Margaret climbed into bed. She lay listening to it for a long time, unable to sleep.

Slowly, to her horror, she began to hear words in the rain, words in her brain, the same words as last night, growing clearer and stronger than ever. *Come to me, Margaret. Please. Oh please come to me.*

"Leave me alone!" she shouted at last.

At least, she thought she shouted it. But since Auntie Alma didn't come in to find out what was wrong, maybe she hadn't shouted it after all. She shuddered. Had the thing, whatever it was, stolen her voice?

She tried again. *"Leave me alone!"*

That sounded real enough. Why didn't Auntie Alma come?

She tried the direct approach. "Auntie Alma! Auntie Alma, I need you!"

No answer. No sound except the falling rain, and the voice that came from within it, calling her name, calling her to the pond.

A cold dread grew inside her. Where was Auntie Alma? Why didn't she come?

Part of her longed to fling aside the covers and go in search of the old woman. Another part of her shrank in terror from the thought of leaving the bed.

She lay, trembling, until the voice finally left her alone. It was hours before she slept.

In the morning, there were puddles of pond water on her floor again. The sight terrified Margaret so thoroughly that she couldn't bring herself to get out of bed until Auntie Alma came to her door to see if she was all right.

"Why didn't you come when I called last night?" asked Margaret angrily.

The round old face wrinkled in dismay. "I'm sorry, child. I must have gone out."

"In the rain?"

"I like the rain. I like the darkness. They're beautiful, really, if you pay attention."

"But I was frightened!"

"I'm sorry, sweetheart," said the old woman. "But really, there isn't any reason to be frightened. No reason at all."

Margaret wished that not being afraid was as easy as Auntie Alma made it sound.

That afternoon she went for a walk in the direction farthest from the pond, following a faint trail that wound through the meadow on the north side of the house. She grew uneasy as she moved between the walls of high grass, and at first she was uncertain why. Then she remembered what lay at the end of the path: the small family cemetery where the last three generations of Jeffersons had been buried. She thought about turning back, but then decided against it. The cemetery wasn't really scary. In fact, it was a nice place to sit and think. She had gone there several times with her cousin Peter last summer, and they had talked about everything that they wanted to do when they grew up.

She reached it now, walking under a thick branch of a low-growing apple tree that nearly blocked the path. It was much as she remembered it: a small clearing—about the same size as the pond, actually—hedged all around with brush and brambles that were starting to creep their way into the cemetery itself.

Fifteen or twenty white stones, some cracked, others severely tilted, marked the haphazardly arranged graves. Wild roses twined over many of the stones, and a variety of flowers grew on and around the low mounds that rose over the final resting places of Auntie Alma's relatives. The old woman had told Margaret that she would probably be the last one to be buried here. She had no children of her own, and none of her nieces and nephews seemed to want a spot here. Margaret thought that was a little sad.

She sat beneath the apple tree and listened

to the birds. The warm sun felt good. After a while she got up and began to read the gravestones, calculating the ages of various Jeffersons when they had died. The set that always got to her was a group of four—mother, father, and two children. What brought a lump to Margaret's throat every time she read the stones was that the husband and children had all died within a year of each other, leaving the mother to live on alone for another fifty years. Her messages on the headstones always struck Margaret as infinitely sad. Carved into each were the words "I will love you forever" with not the woman's name but her relationship (Mother, Mother, Wife) inscribed beneath.

At the south side of the little clearing, she noticed a grave that she didn't remember. The stone was not weathered, and the grave itself was not overgrown as the others were. The skin at the back of her neck prickled as if caterpillars had begun crawling across it.

A horrified feeling growing in her chest, she walked to the grave and knelt to read the stone.

Alma Jefferson, Beloved Friend

And the date—April of this year.
With a cry, Margaret turned and ran from

the cemetery. She raced back along the path, the grass whipping at her legs. Halfway to the house she suddenly stopped. How could she go back there, back to the old woman who was dead?

She had to call her parents, tell them to come and get her.

Only she didn't know where they were.

She stopped. How could they have left her here to begin with?

The world seemed to swirl around Margaret. Finally her fear overwhelmed her, and she blacked out.

When she awoke, it was to the music of crickets singing in the grass. The moon was riding low at the edge of the sky, pale and insubstantial, yet somehow comforting. She remembered her teacher explaining that Shakespeare had had Juliet call the moon "inconstant" because it changed every night, moving through each month from nothing to fullness and back to nothing again. That might be, but at least it always came back. That was constant enough for Margaret right now. Its pale presence was like an old friend.

Like Auntie Alma.

Margaret stood still for a moment, then made up her mind. Auntie Alma had taken good care of her, hadn't tried to hurt her, would never try to hurt her. There was nothing in the house to be afraid of. Maybe the old woman even needed her help.

Telling herself this, ignoring the deeper, stranger questions that fought for her attention, Margaret made her way back to the house.

It was empty.

Somehow she had known that would be the case. Even so, a chill crept over her. Where was Auntie Alma? Or, to be more specific, where had her ghost gone? Margaret had read enough ghost stories to have some idea of how this might work. She feared that her discovery of the tombstone had driven the ghost away.

Leaving her here alone.

Why was she here alone?

It grew darker. Margaret thought about getting something to eat, but her stomach was too tight for that.

And then the calling began again.

Margaret. Mar-gar-et. Come to me. Please, please come to me.

Was it Auntie Alma calling?

No, that couldn't be. It wasn't her voice.

But if it wasn't Auntie Alma, then who was it?

Or what?

The house was too dark and lonely to protect her. The call had grown too strong to resist. She began to cry softly. Against her will, she drifted through the door. With no light save that of the pale moon, she walked through the backyard, past the grape arbor, along the overgrown path, over the ridge to the pond.

Fireflies darted and blinked in the dew-soaked grass, their brief, pale lights flashing on and off. But the crickets had fallen silent, as if waiting for something. No breeze stirred the surface of the water. The moon was in the pond, its reflection like a ghost.

On the other side, standing among the willows, was Auntie Alma, who held out her translucent hands longingly to Margaret, imploring the child to come to her.

"I can't!" wailed Margaret. "I can't, I can't!"

And inside her mind the voice was whispering urgently, *Come to me, Margaret. Please! It's time to stop pretending.*

She walked to the edge of the water, to the same place she had found herself standing again and again over the last few days. The horror was growing, filling her so full it seemed as if she must burst with it.

Auntie Alma called to her from across the pond. "Margaret, the only way out is in."

Margaret stood trembling in the darkness.

"The only way out is in."

What was that supposed to mean? Part of her knew what it meant. Even so, she wanted to ask. But she knew that Auntie Alma couldn't tell her, was bending the rules to say even as much as she had.

Margaret turned and ran, but stopped at the top of the rise.

She turned back. The pond lay black and quiet, the moon's reflection like a single enormous eye in its center. The translucent woman still stood on the far side, waiting for her with open arms.

And from the pond's depths came a call that she could no longer resist.

Slowly, she walked down the hill, back to the edge of the water.

"The only way out is in," whispered Auntie Alma, a whisper that came clearly and distinctly across the dark water as if from another country.

Margaret stepped into the pond.

The water was shockingly cold. The bottom of the pond was slick and silty, just as she remembered from the times her mother had waded in with her when she was little, before she was old enough to refuse. She could almost feel it through her shoes, feel the sliding, sucking mud that squeezed between your toes and tried to hold you down.

She took another step and then another.

She was close to the scary part, the drop-off where the pond plunged to unsuspected depths.

Three more steps and she went over the edge. Down she sank through the dark, cold water. The moon's pale light could not pierce this darkness. And yet somehow she could see. Or perhaps she was guided by the voice, which was calling her more intensely than ever. Not Auntie Alma's voice. The other.

She knew who it was, now.

But she would not give it a name.

Not yet.

At the bottom of the pond, in darkness black and absolute, she found it. A low mound, features obscured by the silt that had drifted over it in the few days that it had been here. She longed to flee. Terror throbbed within her, beating at the walls of her heart, screaming, *Get out, get out, get out!*

But the call was too strong, the need of the voice too aching and desperate. Trapped between need and fear, she hung in the dark water, not certain how much longer she could last here. She had to get out.

The only way out is in. The words tickled at the back of her mind. She knew it was true, knew it was the only answer.

Moving forward, she reached out to brush the silt from the poor, cold thing at the bottom of the pond. A lock of hair floated free, and with an eye that needed no outside light she saw it at last, the face she knew so well, the face she had looked at every morning in the mirror.

Her own dark face, now still in death.

Her wail of despair was lost in the dark water.

Now memory flooded over her, pushing away the lies.

Her parents had not gone off and left her here with Auntie Alma. She had come here herself, running away, hoping to find . . . what? A place to escape, for a time, from the fights—and, even more, from the unbearable hope that they might end, that things might get better, that her mother and father might stop the endless war so they could be a family again.

She had taken the little boat out onto the water, thinking she would be safe in it, held above the pond, separate from it. Positioning herself in the center of the pond, she had tossed the anchor over the side of the boat. But in her anger and despair she had carelessly managed to tangle her foot in the rope.

The anchor had pulled her under and held her down. She had struggled frantically to free herself, but finally the water had filled her lungs and she had drowned here in the pond's cold, dark embrace.

Margaret studied the bloated thing that

had once been her, the body that was hers no longer, and realized that at the moment of death she had gone backward, desperately turning back to the world of the living and refusing to acknowledge the truth of what had happened.

And she had been lying to herself ever since, blocking out the memory of her death by trying to pretend that her parents had brought her here, even though she knew in her heart that the house was empty and Auntie Alma had died earlier this year.

No wonder her parents hadn't come back for her. How could they, not having any idea where she had gone?

And now Auntie Alma was waiting for her on the far shore . . . one ghost calling to another. Margaret tried to go to her but couldn't. She was still trapped here in the cold, dark water.

"The only way out is in," Auntie Alma had said.

And then Margaret knew the way out at last.

Beating back her fear with the knowledge that it was time to move on, she reached forward to embrace the cold, dead flesh of her body. Wrapping her ghostly arms around her own corpse, she pressed herself to herself, accepting the reality of her death, rejecting the desperate lie she had fashioned in her attempt to cling to this world, to this life.

This cold thing was her reality. It was who she was and where she was, and until she accepted that she could never get through to the other side.

Hard—harder than she had tried the other night to press herself into the mattress—she embraced the corpse, pressed herself into it . . .

. . . and burst through the other side.

Suddenly the cold was gone. She felt warm and safe. Light seemed to surround her as she shot to the surface of the pond.

Auntie Alma was standing on the far bank, still waiting for her. The old woman laughed as she saw Margaret emerge from the water, climb onto the bank.

Margaret laughed, too, and laughed even harder to find herself warm and dry.

Auntie Alma reached out to her.

Margaret took the old woman's hand and together they walked out of the willows, up the hill, and into the woods—ready to explore the undiscovered country that lay waiting for them on the other side.

Are you sure you want to go to camp this summer? Really, really sure?

LETTERS FROM CAMP

Al Sarrantonio

Dear Mom and Dad,

I still don't know why you made me come to this dump for the summer. It looks like all the other summer camps I've been to, even if it is "super modern and computerized," and I don't see why I couldn't go back to the one I went to last year instead of this "new" one. I had a lot of fun last summer, even if you did have to pay for all that stuff I smashed up and even if I did make the head counselor break his leg.

The head counselor here is a jerk, just like the other one was. As soon as we got off the hovercraft that brought us here, we had to go to the Big Tent for a "pep talk." They made us sit through a slide show about all the things we're going to do (yawn), and that wouldn't have been so bad except that the head counselor, who's a robot, kept scratching his metal head through the whole thing. I haven't made any friends, and the place looks like it's full of jerks. Tonight we didn't have any hot water and the TV in my tent didn't work.

Phooey on Camp Ultima. Can't you still get me back in the other place?

Dear Mom and Dad,

Maybe this place isn't so bad after all. They just about let us do whatever we want, and the kids are pretty wild. Today they split us up into "Pow-wow Groups," but there aren't really any rules or anything, and my group looks like it might be a good one. One of the guys in it looks like he might be okay. His name's Ramon, and he's from Brazil. He told me a lot of neat stories about things he did at home, setting houses on fire and things like that. We spent all day today hiding from our stupid robot counselor. He thought for sure we had run away and nearly blew a circuit until we finally showed up just in time for dinner.

The food stinks, but they did have some animal-type thing that we got to roast over a fire, and that tasted pretty good.

Tomorrow we go on our first field trip.

★   ★   ★

Dear Mom and Dad,

We had a pretty good time today, all things considered. We got up at six o'clock to go on our first hike, and everybody was pretty excited. There's a lot of wild places here, and they've got it set up to look just like a prehistoric swamp. One kid said we'd probably see a Tyrannosaurus Rex, but nobody believed him. The robot counselors kept us all together as we set out through the marsh, and we saw a lot of neat things like vines dripping green goop and all kinds of frogs and toads. Me and Ramon started pulling the legs off frogs, but our counselor made us stop and anyway the frogs were all robots. We walked for about two hours and then stopped for lunch. Then we marched back again.

The only weird thing that happened was that when we got back and the counselors counted heads, they found that one kid was missing. They went out to look for him but couldn't find anything, and the only thing they think might have happened is that he got lost in the bog somewhere. One kid said he thought he saw a Tyrannosaurus Rex, but it was the same kid who'd been talking about them before, so nobody listened to him. The head counselor went around patting everybody on the shoulder, telling us not to worry since something always happens to one kid every year. But they haven't found him yet.

Tonight we had a big food fight, and nobody even made us clean the place up.

Dear Mom and Dad,

Today we went out on another field trip, and another stupid kid got himself lost. They still haven't found the first one, and some of the kids are talking about Tyrannosaurus Rex again. But this time we went hill climbing and I think the dope must have fallen off a cliff, because the hills are almost like small mountains and there are a lot of ledges on them.

After dinner tonight, which almost nobody ate because nobody felt like it, we sat around a campfire and told ghost stories. Somebody said they thought a lot of kids were going to disappear from here, and that made everybody laugh, in a scary kind of way. I was a little scared myself. It must have been the creepy shadows around the fire. The robot counselors keep telling everyone not to worry, but some of the kids—the ones who can't take it—are starting to say they want to go home.

I don't want to go home, though; this place is fun.

Dear Mom and Dad,

Today we went on another trip, to the far

side of the island where they have a lake, and we had a good time and all (we threw one of the robot counselors into the lake but he didn't sink), but when we got off the boat and everybody was counted we found out that eight kids were gone. One kid said he even saw his friend Harvey get grabbed by something ropy and black and pulled over the side. I'm almost ready to believe him. I don't know if I like this place so much anymore. One more field trip like the one today and I think I'll want to come home.

It's not even fun wrecking stuff around here anymore.

Dear Mom and Dad,

Come and get me right away, I'm *scared*. Today the robot counselors tried to make us go on another day trip, but nobody wanted to go, so we stayed around the tents. But at the chow meeting tonight only twelve kids showed up. That means twenty more kids disappeared today. Nobody had any idea what happened to them, though I do know that a whole bunch of guys were playing outside the perimeter of the camp, tearing things down, so that might have had something to do with it. At this point I don't care.

Just get me out of here!

*   *   *

Mom and Dad,

I think I'm the only kid left, and I don't know if I can hide much longer. The head counselor tricked us into leaving the camp today, saying that somebody had seen a Tyrannosaurus Rex. He told us all to run through the rain forest at the north end of the camp, but when we ran into it, something horrible happened. I was with about five other kids, and as soon as we ran into the forest we heard a high-pitched screeching and a swishing sound and the trees above us started to lower their branches. I saw four of the kids I was with get covered by green plastic-looking leaves, and then there was a gulping sound and the branches lifted and separated and there was nothing there. Ramon and I just managed to dodge out of the way, and we ran through the forest in between the trees and out the other side. We would have been safe for a while but just then the robot counselors broke through the forest behind us, leading a Tyrannosaurus Rex. We ran, but Ramon slipped and fell and the Tyrannosaurus Rex was suddenly there, looming over him with its dripping jaws and rows of sharp white teeth. Ramon took out his box of matches but the dinosaur was on him then and I didn't wait to see any more.

I ran all the way back to the postal computer terminal in the camp to get this letter out to you. Call the police! Call the army! I can't hide forever, and I'm afraid that any second the Tyrannosaurus Rex will break in here and

Dear Mr. and Mrs. Jameson:

Camp Ultima is happy to inform you of the successful completion of your son's stay here, and we are therefore billing you for the balance of your payment at this time.

Camp Ultima is proud of its record of service to parents of difficult boys, and will strive in the future to continue to provide the very best in camp facilities.

May we take this opportunity to inform you that, due to the success of our first camp, we are planning to open a new facility for girls next summer.

We hope we might be of service to you in the future.

Some vampires just won't take "no" for an answer!

VAMPIRE FOR HIRE

Patrick Bone

He didn't want to see it again. Never again! It was the worst nightmare ever. But when he woke and opened his eyes it was still there in the window. So he squeezed his eyes shut, hoping it would go away.

The wind blew hard against the old house. Tree branches slapped at the siding, and something inside the boy said *Don't look again and it will go away.* Finally, he could take no more and ran screaming from his room, racing to his parents for help.

He should have known better.

"You're just dreaming," his dad said in a rigid voice.

"Just this time, Dad, please let me stay in your room," the boy pleaded, his face wet with tears.

His mom even tried to make an exception. "Just one night, Henry, let the kid stay just one night."

But his father was inflexible. "No exceptions! There's no such thing as a vampire."

The boy was frightened and frustrated. But he couldn't blame his father. After all, who could believe a kid who said he was being visited by a vampire?

The next night and every night after that he did not run to his parents when the noises came at the window. Instead, he cried, and when he couldn't hold in the terror, he screamed. At first, his mother came to his room, looked out the window, turned on the lights, checked the closet, looked under the bed. When she found nothing, she tried reasoning with him. "Cuthbert," she said (how could anyone name their child Cuthbert?), "Cuthbert, you're just going through a stage."

But when he finally fell back asleep, the nightmare would start again. And the moment he opened his eyes, the thing he had feared would be there, just as in his nightmare, standing on nothing but air outside his second-story window.

It didn't really look like a vampire, at least not one he had ever seen in the movies. No tuxedo, no cape, not even slick black hair or long canine teeth. But it didn't look human, either.

The face the boy saw in the window was as white as a corpse, with lips so brittle and cracked it seemed as if the creature needed a drink of water, or . . . maybe blood? Then the smell: like death.

Its hair was long and stringy and blew every which way in the wind. The eyes were dull, lifeless, yellow about the iris. The boy was sure he had never seen those eyes blink. A coarse brown robe covered the vampire's body, revealing bare feet almost as bony as the gnarled hands and deformed fingers. His long, twisted fingernails scraped against the windowpane.

Every night Cuthbert fought to keep his eyes closed. With nothing else to get him through, he frantically continued to tell himself that if he couldn't see the vampire, it would go away. But even with his eyes shut, he could hear the fingernails against the window. The boy tried burying his head under the pillow and pulling the covers over that. Nothing helped. He could still hear it scratching against the windowpane, and he could hear the voice. Nothing could smother the sound of that voice.

Every night the vampire would speak to the boy, in low, hollow tones, moaning the

same message as before: "Let me in, Cuthbert. Open the window; let me come in."

The boy's body would turn cold, numb, but he still found the strength to scream, "NO! Go away! Please, go away and leave me alone."

"But you sent for me," the vampire would say. Every night the same message: "Let me in, Cuthbert. You sent for me. It's too late to go back now. Open the window and let me in."

Stupid thing about it was, the boy really had sent for it.

It all started when Cuthbert decided he had to do something about his social standing in school. Actually it was more like his *personal safety* and social standing in school.

He could never figure out why he was picked on so much. It did strike him that having a name like Cuthbert did nothing for his image. He was smaller than the other boys in his class. He wondered if that was why. All he knew for sure was that almost every kid in his class took turns ridiculing him. That was bad, but not as bad as Boris Broadbottom.

Boris Broadbottom got his thrills kicking Cuthbert around the schoolyard. Actually, any yard would do. Didn't matter to Boris. He relished taunting him. "Gonna get you, Cuthbert," he would say. "Any time, any place. Gonna get you!" And he did—regularly.

When Cuthbert complained at home, his dad said he would not tolerate a whiny kid, not his son, no whining, no sir. No exceptions.

His mom said, "There, there, Cuthbert. Boris is just going through a stage. I know, why don't you have him for lunch?"

Cuthbert's mom loved to do lunch. She was sure the world's problems could be solved if everybody would just do lunch. When he tried to tell her boys like Boris Broadbottom don't "do lunch," she said, "Just a stage, Cuthbert. He's just going through a stage. Do have him for lunch."

So now you can understand why Cuthbert was so interested in an ad he read in one of the freebie newspapers floating around town. The ad said:

Tired of being bullied? Sick of being pushed around during recess? Ready to turn the tables and fight back? Then you need: VAMPIRE FOR HIRE.

He copied down the name and address, borrowed an envelope and stamp from his mom's desk, and sent the letter.

A week later, the nightmares started, and Cuthbert got more than he bargained for. He had expected a vampire to do his dirty work for him, not to try to turn *him* into a vampire. But that's not the way vampires operate.

For weeks the horror at his bedroom window continued. Nothing would make the nightmares go away, not even the old close-your-eyes trick. Still, no matter how often it demanded to be let in, the vampire stayed outside the window, never tried to break in, never even attempted to raise the window.

Cuthbert wasn't dumb enough to let it in, either. He remembered something he'd read in an old library book about vampires not being able to come into your house unless you invited them in. He was safe, he hoped, as long as he kept the window shut. It seemed he was right.

Suddenly the nightmares stopped. Just like that, they stopped. No more nightmares, no more vampire, no more wind howling against his bedroom window.

Cuthbert woke up on a Saturday morning and looked outside to see the sun shining. He heard the birds singing, and he was happy because the vampire hadn't come the night before. It was over. He was relieved.

He should have known better. He had also read in the old library book that a vampire never gives up. Where there's a vampire will, the book said, there's a vampire way. Cuthbert was soon to discover there's more than one way for a vampire to invade a home.

Later that day, when Cuthbert was sprawled on the hallway floor playing with his pet turtle, Fuzzball, the doorbell rang.

His mom went to the door. The messenger outside was dressed in a black suit. He said, "Package for Cuthbert." Then he handed her an object wrapped in brown paper and walked away.

When Cuthbert's mom turned around, her mouth sort of hung open as if it had come unhinged from her jaw. The package was about the size of a shirt box. She shook it. She shook it again, this time closer to her ear, then looked at it with her lips pursed to the side and her head cocked. "Very strange," he heard her say. She didn't seem interested in letting Cuthbert know there was a package for him, so he stayed in the hall shadows with Fuzzball and watched her sit on the couch to open the package.

It was a book, a black book as far as he could see. She opened it, turned a page, screamed, slammed it shut, and bolted straight for the garage. He heard the door open and close, then open and close again. It didn't take a detective to figure out she had gone out to the garage to toss *his* book in the trash.

Why is it some kids never learn to leave

well enough alone? He could have forgotten about it, lying in his bed that night with no nightmares to keep him awake. He *should* have forgotten about it.

But he didn't.

It was midnight when he slipped out of bed and tiptoed down the stairs to the garage. When he opened the door, it was pitch black and cold. Something seemed to move behind one of the cars. He knew it couldn't be Fuzz-ball because he had put him away in his terrar-ium for the night—not that the turtle could get into the garage anyway. He listened. Goose-bumps rose over every inch of his body, but he heard nothing. Finally he crept over to the garbage can. For a second, when he reached in and felt through the trash for the book, he thought he saw something glow.

By twelve-fifteen, he was lying on his stomach under the covers of his bed, a flash-light in one hand and the book in the other. On the black leather cover were the words *For-bidden Chants and Spells.*

A sudden gust of wind battered against the window, and he was sure he heard a faraway voice saying, "Don't do it, Cuthbert."

What an imagination! he thought.

Then he laughed. "This is just an old book, not a vampire," he whispered. He tried not to think about his mom screaming when she opened it. Slowly, he balanced the book on the pillow in front of him and opened the cover. Nothing. Just a blank page. He laughed again, this time a nervous laugh, and turned the first page. A shudder went down his back when he saw what was printed in dark, bold letters in the center of the next sheet:

DO NOT TURN THE PAGE

The boy shivered.

"Close the book, Cuthbert," he said to himself. "Close it while you still have time." But his hand reached up and flicked at the edge of the page, tickling it with his finger. "This is just a joke," he said, and turned the page.

He couldn't remember a thing that happened after that.

When Monday morning came, it was cold and rainy. The boy was surprised at how happy he felt. He used to hate the rain. Now it seemed so refreshing. He poked at his oatmeal and his mom said in a worried voice, "Aren't you hungry, dear? You haven't eaten since dinner on Saturday."

It was strange. He felt hungry, but not for oatmeal.

"I'll eat lunch at school," he told her.

*   *   *

Boris Broadbottom sat next to Cuthbert in math class. He made faces and mouthed the words "I'll get you later, sissy boy." Cuthbert could smell Boris' foul breath when the bully whispered, "Any time, any place."

That's when something flashed in Cuthbert's mind and he leaned toward Boris and said, "I just got a great idea, Boris. Why don't we meet under the bleachers in the gym after class? Mom said I should try to make friends; she said I should have you . . . for lunch."

The hardest thing we ever have to do is make up our minds.

ONE CHANCE

Charles de Lint

It was the summer they shared their unhappiness.

Susanna sped down Main Street, standing up on the pedals to get her bike going, the front panels of her khaki army jacket flapping against her arms. The jacket was a couple of sizes too big for her. She had to roll the sleeves up and the waistband hung down around her thighs.

It had belonged to her grandfather and when she'd found it in the attic up at the top of his old house at the beginning of summer, he had given it to her with a sad smile. It was the same smile he'd worn when he fixed up Teddy Baker's old one-speed bike for her. The kind of smile that said, If we weren't so poor . . . The kind of look her parents got sometimes, only they didn't smile.

She knew she looked stupid wearing it, riding her balloon-tire bike. She could see it in the eyes of the people she passed. She heard it from the other kids. "Suzy Four-eyes, get a coat your own size." And Tommy Cothorn asking her if she was an old lady, because she rode an old lady's bike and she sure was too ugly to be a girl.

But she didn't feel stupid wearing it. She felt free in that old jacket, riding her bike. She was an army scout, down behind enemy lines. Whizzing down Main Street, swinging left on Powers without using the brakes, not slowing down at all, just leaning into the corner, so close to the Coca-Cola truck parked there that she could swear she'd brushed the side of the truck with her arm.

She was trying very hard to hold back tears. The bike helped. Air rushing against her face. The rubber hum of its big fat tires on the pavement. The jacket brought her close to her grandfather. It was the same jacket he'd worn when he went overseas. No matter how often it was washed, for her it always smelled like him. Like dry apples and leaves burning in autumn. But her back still hurt from where she'd fallen against the bench in the park when Tommy's brother Bobby pushed her down. And then everybody had laughed as she sat there, trying not to cry, trying to find her glasses, just wanting to get away.

At the corner of Blaylock Avenue and Powers, she steered left into the alleyway beside old man Koontz's junk shop, skimmed between two garbage cans like a circus trick rider, and then she was bumping over the uneven ground of the empty lot behind the grocery store.

Billy was already there.

As she brought her bike to a halt, he turned to look at her, fingers tight around the paperback copy of *Witch Week* that she'd lent him. Her own unhappiness fled when she saw the big smudged bruise on Billy's face. His right eye was so swollen it was almost closed. Laying her bike down, she walked over to where he was sitting. She leaned back against the rear wall of the grocery store as he was doing, and looked out across the lot.

It was hard to be eleven and hold so much unhappiness in such small bodies.

Susanna took off her glasses. The rivets on the left hinge were loose, but they couldn't be tightened anymore. A piece of black tape held the hinge to the temple. She cleaned the lenses on the hem of her jacket, then put the glasses back on. The bridge was a little tight because she was outgrowing them. Her mother had promised her a new pair next year.

"He got real mad last night," Billy said.

He didn't lie to her like he did to everyone else. He didn't say he fell going down the stairs, or he'd walked into a door, or anything like that. His dad went out drinking after work, and sometimes he came home happy, but sometimes he came home and you couldn't say anything to him. One wrong word and his big fist would come as if out of nowhere and send Billy flying halfway across the room. Sometimes it didn't even have to take a wrong word.

"I was just sitting on the couch, reading your book," Billy said, "and he hit me. He didn't say anything, he just hit me. And when I tried to get up, he hit me again. And then he pushed me off the couch and he lay down and he passed out."

There were no tears lying in wait behind Billy's eyes. His voice was flat and even and he just kept on staring out across the lot. But then he turned to look at Susanna.

"If I stay there any longer, he's gonna kill me, or I . . . I'm . . ."

His voice trailed off.

"Bobby Cothorn caught me in the park," Susanna said. She knew what had happened to her wasn't even vaguely on the same level as what happened to Billy, but it was a way of sharing the pain. Sharing their unhappiness.

"I'm going away," Billy said.

Susanna didn't say anything for a long moment.

"You can't," she said finally.

"I've *got* to, Suze," he said. "I can't take it anymore. Not the kids picking on me, not my dad hitting me. School's starting in two weeks. We can hide in places like this in the summer, we can get away from the other kids so they won't hurt us, but what are we gonna do when school starts? We won't be able to hide from them then. And I can't hide from my dad—not unless I go away."

"But you're just a kid," Susanna said, being practical. "Where will you go? How will you live? The cops'll just track you down and bring you back home and then you'll *really* be in trouble."

"I'm going someplace they can't ever find me."

Susanna shook her head. There wasn't anywhere an eleven-year-old could go that he couldn't be found. For an afternoon, sure. But not forever.

"Can't be done," she said.

"What about Judy Lidstone?" he replied.

Susanna shivered. Judy Lidstone had lived just a few blocks from her on Snyder Avenue. She'd disappeared in the spring.

"She didn't run away," Susanna said. "Some

psycho got her. They just ... they just
never—"

"Found her body?"

"Yeah."

"Well, I know different."

"Bull."

Billy shook his head and leaned conspirato-
rially closer. "She went *away*," he said, and
there was something in the way he said "away"
that stopped Susanna cold. She shivered again,
but it was a different kind of a chill that touched
her now. Born not so much of fear as of wonder. At the unknown.

"Where did she go?" she asked.

"I don't know the name of the place, but
I know how to get there. By magic."

The shivery feeling left Susanna. "Oh, get
real," she said. She looked away from him and
began to poke about in a hole in her jeans with
a dirt-smudged finger.

"You've got to have a key to get to that
place," Billy said as though she hadn't spoken.
"You've got to have the right key and you've
got to believe it's going to work. *Really* believe.
And then, if the key works—*when* it works—
you go away."

"Where to?"

"To a better place. Someplace where your
dad doesn't beat on you and kids don't make

fun of you. Where you don't have to ever hide again."

"Who told you this?" Susanna asked.

"Judy did—before she left."

Susanna's shiver returned. Billy looked so serious, so believing, that she couldn't help but wonder—what if it *is* true?

"But you've got to go when the door opens to that other place—right then. You don't get another chance."

"Judy told you?" Susanna said.

Billy nodded.

"And you never told anybody?"

"Who'm I going to tell?" Billy asked. "Who's going to believe me?"

"How come you never told me?"

"I'm telling you now," Billy said.

Susanna took off her glasses and began to clean them again, lingering over the job. To go away. To go to a place where no one dumped on you. If it was possible . . .

"Remember, Judy disappeared from her room in the middle of the night?" Billy asked. "Well, how's some psycho going to get into her house without waking her parents? No. She told me about the key before she went, and she told me where she'd leave it. I thought it was just a load of bull. But then she *did* disappear, so I figured it had to be true. I went into her backyard and the key was lying there in back behind her dad's toolshed—just like she said it would be."

"What does it look like?"

Billy laid her book on the ground between them and pulled a brass object from his pocket—a figurine of a wolf, so tarnished it almost looked like bronze. He gave it a rub on the knee of his jeans, then passed it over to Susanna. It didn't look like any kind of key she had ever seen before.

"How does it work?" she asked.

"He's like the guy who guards the door," Billy said, stroking the figurine. "You've got to hold this real tight and call him. And you've got to believe he'll come. . . ."

Susanna nodded slowly, almost to herself. "When . . . when are you going?" she asked.

"Now, Suze. Right now. Are you coming?"

"I—"

Susanna thought of Bobby Cothorn and his pals catching her in the park, pushing her back and forth between them. "You better hope you grow into a beautiful bod," someone had said, "because with a face like yours, you'll need all the help you can get." With a face like hers. Mouth too big, teeth crooked. Ears sticking out. She didn't need a mirror to tell her she was ugly. All she had to do was to look in somebody's eyes. Anybody's.

"I'll come," she said.

Billy grinned, his swollen eye giving his face a strange cast. "All *right*," he said.

"So what do we do?" Susanna added.

Billy scrambled to his feet. "We call him," he said, tapping his chest. "In here. And we have to really *believe* he's going to come."

Somewhat doubtfully, Susanna got to her feet as well. "Just like that?"

"It's got something to do with how badly we need to get away," Billy said. "At least that's what Judy said. All I know is that we only get the one chance."

He turned away and stared at the middle of the lot, brow furrowed with concentration. Susanna looked at him for a moment, then let her gaze follow his.

There was something too simple about this, she thought. Didn't magic have to be more complicated? This was something anybody could do. Except, she answered herself, you had to have the wolf figurine first. You had to have the key.

If anybody else had told her about this, she'd have thought, *Yeah. Sure. And you better be good 'cause Santa was watching you.* But this was Billy. Billy didn't go in for that kind of stuff. He was tough. Too small to stand up to the bigger kids when they wanted to dump on someone, but tough enough to take it when it was dished out. He didn't run home and cry.

No, Susanna thought. Because what was waiting at home for him was ten times worse than what he'd get in the schoolyard.

So—a wolf. She was game to call him. She felt sort of goofy doing it, but if the wolf could do a Peter Pan and take them away . . .

She felt Billy trembling beside her and flicked her eyes open, not even able to remember when she'd shut them. She looked at Billy, realizing that she'd *felt* him tremble, except he was still standing a few feet away. It was as though the air had moved between their bodies, set into motion by the shiver of his skin to tickle hers. She could see him shake now, hands tight at his sides, trembling.

A funny look had come over his face. A happy look. She wondered if she'd ever seen him look this happy before—just dreamy, relaxed—happy. She was about to call his name when she heard a faint thrumming in the air. Then she realized that Billy wasn't just concentrating on calling the wolf—he was seeing something, out there in the middle of the lot.

Slowly she turned to see what it was. She thought she'd die.

There, in the middle of the lot, standing in amongst the weeds and broken bottles and refuse, was the biggest dog she'd ever seen. No. Not a dog. It had to be a wolf. *The* wolf. Its grizzled hackles were bushy like a lion's mane.

Its chest was deep, its head broad. And its eyes . . . they were the color of a Siberian husky's, but this was no husky. This was something wild. Feral. With its crystal-blue eyes that were like bright sunlight coming through an icicle.

Billy turned to her with shining eyes. "Oh, Suze . . ." His voice was a whispering breath.

Susanna nodded. It had come. She started to grin, but something was happening with the wolf. It was . . . changing. Standing on its hind legs now, nose lifted high, its body began to shift and change—until what stood out there in the empty lot was some hybrid creature, part man, part wolf.

Oh, jeez, Susanna thought. *It's the wolf-man from the late night* Creature Feature *movies.*

She took a nervous step back. Maybe she hadn't really believed, but Billy sure had and something—

(had to be a trick)

—had come. There it stood, something that shouldn't have been possible. But it wasn't scary—not like in the movies. Its eyes . . . they were distant-cool and warm all at the same time. You could get lost in those eyes. They promised relief from every pain. They could heal anything. Except the world didn't work that way, did it? There weren't any easy ways out—were there?

(had to be a trick)

Any minute now, the Cothorn brothers and some of their pals were going to come out from behind the fence on the other side of the lot, laughing and pointing at them. The wolfman was going to deflate because it—

(had to be a trick)

—was just a balloon. Or a cardboard cutout. A trick.

Except the wolfman really moved, and behind it now, opening like one of those futuristic doors in a science-fiction movie that worked like a camera shutter, was an oval window into another world. Through that gap in the air they could see green fields unrolling under a blue sky, the colors so bright they hurt the eye. It—

(had to be a trick)

—was a mirage or a hallucination. Because there weren't wolfmen and if there were, they'd be in a zoo or a laboratory somewhere. And there was no such thing as magic, except for special effects in movies, and that was all tricks. And there weren't other worlds that you could just step into through a hole in the air. Except—

Billy took her arm. "Come on, Suze," he said, and he began to lead her toward the wolfman with its crystal eyes filled with promise. And now she could smell the world beyond it,

a clean rich scent that was all good smells—autumn leaves burning, roses in summer, lilac blossoms in spring—all mixed together. The air that came wafting out of that hole in the air, from that otherworld, was so pure and clean, you could almost see the difference between it and the tired old air of the lot.

They were going to step right in through that hole, Susanna thought. The wolfman was already turning, stepping gracefully over the lip, one hairy foot in that impossibly green grass, the other still in the dull end-of-summer weeds of the lot. It turned to look back, to make sure they were following.

They reached the hole in the air and Susanna pulled free of Billy's grip.

"Suze?" he said, confused. He looked from her to the land through the gateway. Was the gateway getting smaller already?

"Don't you see?" Susanna said. "It—"

(has to be a trick)

"—can't be real."

Billy backed away from her. "No," he said, shaking his head. The bruise on his face was like a dark accusation. "Don't say that, Suze."

She knew what he saw—years of hiding from school bullies, of beatings from his father. At least she had her family. But she saw . . . What did she see? That she was as scared of this as she was of everything else? Of leaving her house, because the other kids would dump on her? Of walking down the school halls to sniggers and laughter?

She wanted to believe that it was real. Billy stepped over the lip of the gateway. Behind him the wolfman watched her, a sad look in its blue eyes. Like the look in her grandfather's eyes when he'd given her his old jacket. Like the look in her parents' eyes when they'd tried to explain why she had to do without new glasses, or braces to straighten her crooked teeth, or all the other things they couldn't afford.

She wanted to believe, but she couldn't shake the fear that it was a trick. That she would step toward it, try to cross over, and then the laughter would start. All that endless laughter that was worse than being pushed or getting hit.

There came a humming in the air and she could see the sides of the gateway shimmering as they closed.

All I know is we only get the one chance, she heard Billy say in her mind.

She reached forward, she took a step closer, then hesitated again. This wasn't right. Maybe it wasn't a trick. Maybe the wolfman and that land through the gateway really *was* real. But it wasn't right. Maybe for Billy it was, but not for her. You didn't run away from your problems. That was what her parents said. And Granddad, too. When she thought of her parents, and of the hurt that would be in her grandfather's eyes . . . That wasn't the way you treated those you loved. She was scared to go, sure; but more than that, she knew it would be wrong for her to run away.

So she let them go, Billy and the wolfman, running through those green fields. Just before the gate closed she saw that they were both wolves now, one big and one small, gamboling like puppies. Then the gateway was gone and she was standing all alone in the middle of the lot with a ringing in her ears. She moved through the spot where the gateway had been, but there was nothing there now. No gateway. No otherworld. But no Billy either.

She bent down and picked up the brass figurine. For one moment it seemed to shift in her hand, from wolf, to man, to wolf again. It was still warm from Billy's grip. It hadn't been a trick after all.

"B-Billy?" she called.

The tears she'd kept at bay earlier this afternoon came welling up behind her eyes in a flood.

One chance, she thought she heard Billy say, but his voice was distant and very far away, like an echo. From an otherworld. *That's all.*

Loneliness settled in her and made her chest hurt. The emptiness of the weedy lot seemed to mock her decision, but she knew she'd done the right thing. The right thing. Why did doing the right thing have to hurt so much sometimes?

Bowing her head, she dropped the figurine into the dirt for someone else to find—someone who could use it, like she couldn't. No. Like she wouldn't. She turned away and shuffled slowly toward her bike. Pulling it up from the ground, she started to wheel it away, then turned for one last look.

"Say hello to . . . to Judy for me, Billy," she called softly.

And then she was standing up on the pedals, pumping away, tears shining in her eyes and dribbling down her cheeks and onto her jacket. The bike jumped across the field and the alleyway swallowed her whole.

Sometimes killing a monster isn't the smartest thing to do.

GRENDEL

Mary Frances Zambreno

The blazing afternoon sun made Sammy squint, but he was too excited to care. He hung over the railing of the wooden observation platform and looked down with fascinated intensity at the large reptile lying half in, half out of the Pacific Ocean. If *only* he could go closer! But Uncle Leonard had told him not to bother the dissection crew—or anyone else. If he did, he would have to go home, and that was to be avoided at all costs. He was lucky to get this close.

It was a *very* large reptile. Stretched out on the ground, it was longer than a semi-trailer, with a head the size of a Volkswagen Beetle. Though definitely lizardlike, from Sammy's point of view it looked more than anything else like the carcass of a big dog covered with ants.

The workers swarming over the huge, scaled form wore yellow hard hats, and face masks to keep from breathing in the odor of rotting flesh.

Up on the platform the smell wasn't so bad. Men and women in khaki jackets took measurements and spoke to each other in clipped, professional voices. One of them was Uncle Leonard, his long face flushed like it was when he got annoyed about something. He was talking to a short man with blond hair and round glasses. The man shook his head. Then both men turned and seemed to look straight at him.

Sammy blinked. "Is something wrong, Uncle Len? You look kind of mad."

"What? No, nothing's wrong," his uncle said. He glanced down at the dissection crews. "Not with you, anyway, Sam. I was just telling my friend Dr. Porter here that the saurian shouldn't have been killed. We could have learned so much from it alive. . . ."

"They've almost got the forearms off now," Sammy said with enthusiasm. "The bones are as big as the ones in the museum."

"They should be," Dr. Porter said, smiling absently. "Now, Leonard, you've got to be reasonable. I mean, look at it! Would you want something like that running around in *your* backyard?"

"The California Shoreline Wildlife Preserve is not anyone's 'backyard,' " Leonard said stiffly. "It's a limited-access wilderness area intended for scientific study. Of all the places that a prehistoric survival might have come ashore, the preserve was probably the safest."

"Tell that to the three campers and the fisherman it mangled," Dr. Porter said, wiping his forehead with the back of one hand. "Look, Leonard, I know you're upset about what happened to Godzilla—"

"And I wish you wouldn't use that ridiculous name," Leonard broke in. "What if the press should pick up on it?"

"Oh, lighten up, will you?" Dr. Porter said, rolling his eyes. "It's just a joke."

"It's demeaning," Leonard said pettishly. "One of the most significant finds of the century—of any century—shouldn't be referred to as if it were a refugee from a bad movie."

Dr. Porter shrugged. "So, if you don't like Godzilla, call it Grendel. That's highbrow enough for anyone."

"Grendel?" Leonard asked, raising his eyebrows.

"You know, from *Beowulf*. Come on, Leonard, you must have heard of *Beowulf*."

"Of course I've heard of *Beowulf*," Leonard said defensively. "I simply don't recollect ever having read it, that's all. I'm a scientist, not an English major."

"Uncle Len?" Sammy said tentatively. "I've read *Beowulf*."

"You have?" his uncle asked, startled. "When?"

"In that honors English class I took last year," he said, trying not to squirm. "The teacher said it was a modernized version, but it was okay. Better than some of the junk we had to read."

"Well, young man, since you apparently know more about English literature than your highly educated paleontologist uncle, suppose you tell him who Grendel was," Dr. Porter said, obviously enjoying himself.

Sammy glanced sideways at his uncle. "He was this monster who used to sneak out at night and kill people."

"What happened to him?" Leonard asked, sounding genuinely curious.

"Well, for a long time he just kept coming and no one could stop him," Sammy said, warming to his story. "Then Beowulf heard about it—he was sort of like Arnold Schwarzenegger, the best fighter around anywhere, and he came to help. He ripped off Grendel's arm, and that killed him."

All three looked down at the dissection crew, now busily separating the reptile's left forearm from its body.

"I think Grendel would be a good name

for the dinosaur," Sammy offered. "Better than Godzilla."

"Anything's better than Godzilla," Leonard said, dismissing the subject. "It doesn't need a name. It *needed* a scientific classification as a living animal. We don't know where it came from, how it survived when all the other giant saurians didn't—where it's been living all these years—we don't know anything!"

"I tell you, we had to kill it," Dr. Porter said. "The thing *ate* people."

"Dr. Porter?" called one of the scientists taking measurements from a few feet away; she had a scanning instrument in her hands, and she was looking at it in confusion. "I'm getting something really strange on the 'scope."

"What does it look like?" Dr. Porter asked, hurrying over. Leonard and Sammy followed him. "Don't tell me the monster is still breathing."

"Oh, no, no, nothing like that," the woman assured him. "I was testing the finder—had it pointed at the horizon, when . . . well, look."

She handed the scanner to Dr. Porter. "That is one weird-looking undersea bulge," Dr. Porter said. "Leonard? What do you think?"

"Could be a whale," Leonard said dubiously. "No, it's too big for a humpback—too big for a blue, even. How fast is it moving?"

"Pretty fast, I'd say. Hard to tell exactly with just the 'scope."

Sammy looked out to sea. The water was roiling strangely, rolling in long unnatural swells under the hot California sun. Something stirred in the back of his mind. "Uncle Len—"

"Not now, Sam, I'm busy."

"But Uncle Len—look!" Sammy pointed.

Irritated, Leonard glanced at the water and froze. Next to him, Dr. Porter whistled.

The waters parted, and up lifted the largest, ugliest head that had ever been seen outside of a Japanese movie. It was fully the size of a house, with a piglike nose set between tusks the size of telephone poles. Scales glittered wetly as it heaved itself half out of the surf, revealing a body large enough to match the head. Most frightening of all was the personality in the slitted yellow eyes that roved the shoreline, the intelligence seeking and searching—and then finding—the partially dismembered corpse.

The great mouth opened, and the creature howled, a keening, grieving wail that lifted and fell like the tide.

"I just remembered, Uncle Len," Sammy said, gulping. "In the book, Grendel had a mother. . . ."

Who better to spin a sea story than a sailor and his wife? Jim and Debra tell me this story was inspired by a figurehead they saw at Mystic Seaport. You can almost smell the salt air as you read this yarn.

JENNY NETTLES

Debra Doyle and
James D. Macdonald

On October the fourth in the year 1773, the brigantine *Jenny Nettles*, merchantman out of New Bedford, made port. No sooner was she tied up than the crew was at work with block and tackle, with hammer and chisel, unshipping the figurehead.

They lifted it up and swung it ashore, the carved and painted wooden statue of a woman in Highland garb, and laid it down on the pier. Then six men on either side they carried it shoulder high to the nearest churchyard. They dug a grave, lowered the figurehead in, and said the words from the Book. When they were done, they filled in the grave, set up crosses at head and foot, and returned to the ship without a word.

None of the crew ever shipped in *Jenny Nettles* again, and more than one of them left the sea for good after that voyage. But not a soul among them would ever say why.

She was built in Halifax in 1755, and christened *Jenny Fraser*.

The owner was a Scotsman, a Fraser of Strathglass. In the bloody year of '45, when the Scottish clans rose up against the crown of England, John Fraser was a new-married man. With a wife to keep, and a child on the way, he stayed out of the fighting. He obtained a certificate of immunity—an official paper showing that he had never fought against King George II—and after the uprising ended in bitter defeat for the rebels at the Battle of Culloden, he trusted in the certificate to protect him from King George's soldiers.

But the redcoat troops who came through Glenmoriston and Strathglass cared nothing for a scrap of paper. He was a Highlander, and that was enough. He was taken prisoner as a rebel and a traitor, and sent to the hulks—the prison ships anchored in the river Thames.

There he remained for the best part of a year, while he and the hundreds of others who

shared the rotting holds of the prison ships grew thinner by the day, until their bones could all be seen. Many died. The corpses were removed only when enough of them had accumulated to make it worthwhile to hire beggars to haul them out.

After an endless time when the only light he saw was a square patch of blue in the deck above, John Fraser and his fellow prisoners were haled out on deck, divided into groups of twenty, and forced to choose lots. One man in each twenty was hanged. The rest were transported—sent to England's colonies in America, with no hope of ever returning home.

John Fraser had come to Halifax unwillingly, but he prospered there as he had never done in his native Scotland. In time he became a wealthy merchant. But he never forgot the wife and child he had lost when King George's soldiers came killing and looting their way through Glen Cannich. And when he built his first ship, it was christened *Jenny Fraser* in his wife's name.

Jenny Fraser was a sweet sailer and had lucky passages, bringing good fortune to her owner and to those who sailed in her. But the time came when John Fraser died in Halifax— of weariness after a hard life as much as from any mortal illness—and the *Jenny* passed into other hands.

*   *   *

In 1764, *Jenny Fraser* was sold for the first time, and in 1768 she was sold again. The first buyer kept the old name, seeing no point in changing what the ship had done well with; but the second, a New Bedford Yankee, had no great liking for another merchant's name on a thing that was his. Nor did he care for wasting ceremony on an object of wood and hemp and canvas. He had the old name painted over and a new one lettered on the sternboard, all without a proper christening, and the ship was called *Jenny Nettles* from that day on.

By 1773, when she left Liverpool for New Bedford with a cargo of Irish linen, fine china, and cotton manufactured goods, no one aboard the brigantine remembered that she had ever been called anything else.

Halfway through the voyage, the wind died.

On the same day, a white bird flew out of the east and circled the *Jenny*'s mainmast three times, crying mournfully. The crew saw it and began to mutter among themselves. Some of them were restless in their minds already, since the owner had put a new captain over them for this voyage.

His name was Pym—a dour man—from Suffolk in England, thickset and grizzle-haired.

Captain Pym had come to the sea later in life instead of being brought up to it from boyhood like most of the *Jenny's* crew. He had a scar on one cheek, like a saber cut, making some people guess that he'd taken the king's shilling in his days as a landsman, and had fought in King George's wars. Perhaps it was for this reason that he was not greatly loved by the common sailors—or perhaps it was only that he was not a New Bedford man.

When no wind had blown for three days, the crew began to speak of ill luck and weather-witches.

"There was a time," said Big Tom, the foretopman, "that I shipped on a vessel with a Finnlander aboard. He said he was German—sometimes he said he was Dutch—but that was a lie; he was a Finn. He kept all the winds of the world in a little leather bag, and he could let 'em out or keep 'em in as he had the desire."

"Are you saying there's a Finnlander among us?" asked another sailor.

"No—we're all New Bedford men. But if I wanted to see home again, I'd look for a bag of wind."

And look they did. But no bag of wind did they find, even though they searched the *Jenny* from truck to keel, save only the captain's cabin, and shifted all her ballast stones.

On the fifth day, the sun rose pale through fog. Not a whisper of wind came to ripple the surface of the ocean, or to blow the mist away.

"It's time one of us did something," said Big Tom. He strode back to the *Jenny's* mainmast and stuck his knife into the wood.

Captain Pym loomed up out of the fog behind him. "What is this mummery, sirrah?"

Big Tom wasn't a man to show fear, even of the captain. "There's bad luck on board," he said, "and I'll do something about it if I can."

The captain looked at him, scowling. "Will you, then?"

"Aye," said Tom, undaunted. "If sticking my knife into the mast doesn't bring us a wind, then I'll whistle out loud until we get one."

"You do that, Tom," the captain said. "You just do that. Mind you don't find more wind than you wanted."

Captain Pym turned and walked aft again. Big Tom waited until the captain was gone back to his cabin, then went on forward, padding on bare, calloused feet along the fog-wet deck. He made his way out onto the *Jenny's* bowsprit, holding on to her forestay as he went.

When Big Tom was as far out on the bowsprit as he could get, he held on to the stay with one hand and commenced to whistle. He whistled until his lips grew raw and his throat grew sore, while below him the water heaved low and oily, and the ship barely moved in the thick groundswell.

After a while, he paused to take breath. And in the silence, he heard a voice—a woman's voice, when he knew there was no woman aboard—speaking from someplace close behind him:

"It'll do ye nae good."

Tom turned and looked, but he saw no one. Once again he started whistling, and again, the woman's voice said:

"It'll do ye nae good."

He looked again, but still he saw no one there. He wet his lips and swallowed hard and began to whistle for a third time. This time he whistled hymn tunes—he who hadn't darkened a church door since he'd gone to sea. And a third time the woman's voice said to him:

"I tell ye truly, man, it'll do ye nae good at a'."

The calm dragged on. Every knife aboard was stuck in the *Jenny's* mainmast, but still they had no wind. The fog that wrapped itself about the brigantine was thick and dirty-looking, like uncarded wool. And by the seventh day, there was no fresh water left aboard.

"There's a full tun of water in the after-hold," said Big Tom, when the ship's cook brought the word to the crew.

"Taste it yourself," said the cook. "It's all salt."

"How did seawater get into the water casks?"

"I didn't say it was seawater," the cook told him. "I said that it was salt."

Two days passed after the *Jenny* ran out of fresh water. The bottom of the scuttlebutt was all of green moss, and no water remained in the barrel for the dipper to scoop up.

"How long will a man live without water?" asked the ship's boy.

"Six days," said Big Tom. "Sometimes eight. Most of 'em go mad first, or drink seawater, and that kills 'em."

"Seawater?"

"Aye. It's poison, you know—full of the devil's salt. But men drink it sometimes, when the thirst is on 'em."

He turned back to the rail, looking off into the glowing fog. The ship creaked as it rolled in the swell, but no waves disturbed the flat calm.

On the fourth day after the water ran out, the *Jenny's* sails dripped with moisture—but it was salt, a bitter brine, and impossible to drink. A faint green mold grew on everything, on the masts and shrouds, on the sails, even on the sailors' clothes, and at night the sails shone with a sickly phosphorescent sheen.

At three bells of the midwatch, with the starboard watch on deck, the fog was as thick as ever. The ship's boy was on the lookout, but on this night there was nothing to see: no stars overhead, no horizon, only the clammy fog wrapping all around them. The darkness was black indeed, as dark high above the deck as locked in the lower hold, and he'd needed to find his way up to the masthead by feel.

All the *Jenny's* sails were set, but they hung limp and useless in the flat calm, waiting for a wind that never came. Then, off to port, the ship's boy saw a light—not a natural light, but the bluish glow of St. Elmo's fire, hovering near the end of the yard.

"On deck!" the boy shouted. "On deck, ahoy!"

No answer came from below, and the fog swallowed his words. Out in the darkness the light shone, pale blue and beckoning. He knew that he shouldn't do it, but he took hold of the yard, swung down to the footropes, and made his way outboard. The light on the yard's end grew larger and larger the closer he came, until at last he saw that it wasn't St. Elmo's fire at all, but a woman sitting and weeping, holding a tiny bundle of cloth in her lap.

The woman looked up, and he saw the tears streaming down her face.

"Who'll gi' me back my bonnie wee bairn?" she asked—the boy lost his grip on the fog-slick jackstay and fell.

Big Tom found the ship's boy by stumbling over him in the dark. The lad had broken his back in his fall from the yard, and it took him some hours to die. During the whole time, he raved in his pain, talking of murdered women and burnt-out farms and laughing soldiers with bloody swords.

Toward the last he grew quiet. At eight bells of the day watch he was buried at sea, wrapped in a piece of sailcloth with forty feet of chain sewed at his feet.

On the morning after his death, a clear fluid began to leak from the *Jenny's* mainmast: slow, glistening droplets that curled out and ran downward from where the knives were stuck in the wood.

"It's water," said the ship's cook. "But not fresh. Salt. Like blood."

"Not like blood," said Big Tom, who had also tasted it. His cheeks were sunken, and his eyes were hollow and dark. "Not like blood— like tears."

*　　*　　*

Captain Pym came from his cabin at last, at six bells of the forenoon watch, with a brace of pistols in his hands.

He'd tasted no water for five days, either, for the *Jenny's* water casks were held in common, but he'd kept wine and whisky enough in his cabin that thirst wasn't what had driven him mad. His eyes were red-rimmed and his face unshaven, and he wore about his neck a bit of polished silver hanging from a chain—the badge of a sergeant in King George's redcoat army.

He staggered forward through the fog, past the waist where the ship's boy had fallen, past the mainmast stuck with knives and the slow tears weeping from the wood, out past the windlass and catheads and up to the very peak of the bow. There he climbed out on the chains, beneath the bowsprit, and stood face-to-face with the brigantine's figurehead—the greater-than-life-sized carving of a young woman dressed in tartan cloth that stood on the *Jenny's* cutwater, her painted gray eyes staring ever outward.

"Damn you!" the captain cried. "Stop the dreams!"

He fired one of his pistols into the figurehead's breast. For a moment longer he stood there with the powder smoke hanging about him. No wind stirred the air to carry it away.

At last he said in a low, almost sobbing voice, "How many times do I have to kill you before you'll stay dead?"

And with that word he placed the muzzle of the second pistol beneath his jaw and fired. His body fell down and away into the still water.

The report of the shot had hardly died, muffled in the heavy fog, before the crew of the *Jenny* heard the distant roaring of the coming wind.

Faint at first, then loud, the wind came nearer and nearer, rushing in at them with fearful speed until the ship heeled over as it struck—a gale so strong that it ripped the last shreds of fog away and bellied the sails, which had so long hung limp, so that the canvas stood out full and fair.

The fog had scattered, but black clouds covered the sky. A thunderbolt cracked. An instant later the rain began pelting down, a torrent of fresh sweet water that filled all the catchment basins on the cabin roof and washed away the smells of brine and thirst.

Lashed by the wind, the ocean—only a moment ago so flat and still—broke into foaming spray. The *Jenny's* bow wave curled up in a froth of white as the wind drove her onward.

The captain's body passed down the port

side before fading from sight astern. After it had vanished completely, a white seabird circled three times around the mainmast of the brigantine *Jenny Nettles*—once named *Jenny Fraser*, after a young woman who had been killed by King George's soldiers outside a burning cottage on the dark slopes of Glen Cannich—and then flew away again into the darkening west.

THOSE THREE WISHES

Judith Gorog

No one ever said that Melinda Alice was nice. That wasn't the word used. No, she was clever, even witty. She was called—never to her face, however—Melinda Malice. Melinda Alice was clever and cruel. Her mother, when she thought about it at all, hoped Melinda would grow out of it. To her father, Melinda's very good grades mattered.

It was Melinda Alice, back in the eighth grade, who had labeled the shy, myopic new girl "Contamination" and was the first to pretend that anything or anyone touched by the new girl had to be cleaned, inoculated, or avoided. High school had merely given Melinda Alice greater scope for her talents.

The surprising thing about Melinda Alice was her power; no one trusted her, but no one avoided her either. She was always included,

81

always in the middle. If you had seen her, pretty and witty, in the center of a group of students walking past your house, you'd have thought, "There goes a natural leader."

Melinda Alice had left for school early. She wanted to study alone in a quiet spot she had because there was going to be a big math test, and Melinda Alice was not prepared. That A mattered; so Melinda Alice walked to school alone, planning her studies. She didn't usually notice nature much, so she nearly stepped on a beautiful snail that was making its way across the sidewalk.

"Ugh. Yucky thing," thought Melinda Alice, then stopped. Not wanting to step on the snail accidentally was one thing, but now she lifted her shoe to crush it.

"Please don't," said the snail.

"Why not?" retorted Melinda Alice.

"I'll give you three wishes," replied the snail evenly.

"Agreed," said Melinda Alice. "My first wish is that my next"—she paused a split second—"my next thousand wishes come true." She smiled triumphantly and opened her bag to take out a small notebook and pencil to keep track.

Melinda Alice was sure she heard the snail say, "What a clever girl," as it made it to the safety of an ivy bed beside the sidewalk.

During the rest of the walk to school, Melinda was occupied with wonderful ideas. She would have beautiful clothes. "Wish number two, that I will always be perfectly dressed," and she was just that. True, her new outfit was not a lot different from the one she had worn leaving the house, but that only meant Melinda Alice liked her own taste.

After thinking awhile, she wrote, "Wish number three. I wish for pierced ears and small gold earrings." Her father had not allowed Melinda to have pierced ears, but now she had them anyway. She felt her new earrings and shook her beautiful hair in delight. "I can have anything: stereo, tapes, TV videodisc, moped, car, anything! All my life!" She hugged her books to herself in delight.

By the time she reached school, Melinda was almost an altruist; she could wish for peace. Then she wondered, "Is the snail that powerful?" She felt her ears, looked at her perfect blouse, skirt, jacket, shoes. "I could make ugly people beautiful, cure cripples . . ." She stopped. The wave of altruism had washed past. "I could pay people back who deserve it!" Melinda Alice looked at the school, at all the kids. She had an enormous sense of power. "They all have to do what *I* want now." She walked down the crowded halls to her locker. Melinda Alice could be sweet, she could be witty. She could—The bell rang for homeroom. Melinda Alice stashed her books, slammed the locker shut, and just made it to her seat.

"Hey, Melinda Alice," whispered Fred. "You know that big math test next period?"

"Oh, no," grimaced Melinda Alice. Her thoughts raced; "That damned snail made me late, and I forgot to study.

"I'll blow it," she groaned aloud. "I wish I were dead."

Everyone knows that kids change when they get to be teenagers. But some changes are bigger than others. . . .

WHAT'S A LITTLE FUR AMONG FRIENDS?

Sherwood Smith

"Come on, guys," I said, looking at Tomi, Chas, and Erika. We were squashed into a corner of the school cafeteria. "Let's get together after school today. We've hardly done anything together lately. I'll get a video from my dad's store—something really terrible that we can laugh over."

"Can't, Alys," Tomi said, flinging her long, black hair over her shoulder. "I've got Swim Club practice today."

"Me, either," Chas said, his round, freckled face wincing at the crash of dishes behind us. "Film Club meeting for me."

"But *we* can watch a film," I protested.

"Sorry, Alys. We're learning how to edit

85

videotape," he said. "It's not quite the same thing."

Erika looked from one of us to the other, her eyes big and solemn behind her glasses. The four of us lived in the same apartment building, and we had been friends since grammar school—my dad called us the Fearsome Foursome. But though he'd also given me the lecture on How Things Change when you hit junior high, I hated seeing us pulled apart by new interests. I liked things the way they had always been.

I sighed and said to Erika, "I guess it's just you and me—"

"I can't," she whispered, ducking her head.

Tomi, Chas, and I stared at small, pale Erika, whose face was half hidden by her dark frizzy hair. She sneaked a quick peek upward, then hunched down even more. "Have to meet someone. Help them with a project."

"Really?" Chas said, looking vaguely surprised that Erika would have anyone outside of our group to meet. Usually she didn't even *talk* to anyone else. She and I'd been best friends since we were five, and she'd always followed my lead. She used to play with the others only if I had to help my dad at the video store. They'd always liked her, though—when she wasn't feeling shy she was fun, and funny, and had the wildest imagination of the four of us.

But around other people she was very shy, and no one else at school had ever bothered to find out these things about her.

Who could she be meeting? Who could she *know*?

"Is it anything I can help with?" I asked.

Erika opened her mouth, but just then the bell rang. She jumped up.

"Erika," I said, "how long will it take? How come you haven't—"

Erika didn't say anything, but she gave me this *look*, her dark eyes behind those thick glasses suddenly, well, *spooky*. I felt my mouth fall open, and before I could shut it, she disappeared in the mass of students shoving their way out of the cafeteria.

Erika's spooky look was still on my mind that night as I ran my bath. Southern California's hot, dry Santa Ana winds were blowing, and I'd opened the window to let out some of the heat that had built up all day. The leaves from the few trees in our cement world skittered along the sidewalks with a sound like claws rattling, giving our shabby, familiar old building an eerie atmosphere, as if the place had been picked up and set down somewhere unreal. I leaned out and looked down toward Erika's lit window, remembering the fun the four of us used to have pretending that the complex was a fortress—how we made up signal codes to use in our windows at night.

As I watched Erika's window, I felt sad. When we were little, we used to have such great times making up stories and acting them out. Erika made up some of the most interesting ones—many of them based on the strange, magic-filled folk tales her grandmother had told her. I knew her interests hadn't changed that much. She liked writing stories, same as I did. So why was she pulling away?

Just then a shadow moved across Erika's curtains. Only for an instant, and it wasn't repeated. Silhouettes of people's heads are sort of lightbulb shaped, but this silhouette was a wedge, like a dog shape.

I blinked, rubbing my eyes under my glasses. Erika's grandmother, a tiny lady from Hungary and—except for my dad—the most honest person I'd ever met, would never let Erika break the apartment building rules and sneak in an animal.

So whose dog?

Help them with a project, Erika had said. *Them*. Not *her*. A boy? A boyfriend that Erika didn't want to tell me about? A whole lot of weird emotions whirled through my head as I kept watching Erika's window. The desert wind had turned chilly, the full moon riding high in the sky. But her window stayed open, her curtains gently blowing in and out.

Finally Dad banged on the door. "Alyssa, will you hurry up in there?"

When my dad was finished, I crept back to the bathroom. Erika's window was still lit. I heard the rhythmic click of toenails on cement, and I glimpsed a long, canine shadow running alongside the building. A *big* canine.

Then a teenaged boy's voice called softly: "Erika?" I felt something weirdly compelling about the voice. "You still here?"

The canine lifted its head, as if listening. Moonlight gleamed in yellow eyes as the beast looked around. I ducked out of sight, the hairs on the back of my neck prickling.

"Erika," the voice called again. "Harmon's nowhere around this place. He took off that way."

And a moment later came Erika's voice— soft and low, but instantly familiar. "Okay, Cameron," she said. "Had to check. But you better go before someone in this building sees you."

Her voice echoed strangely around the courtyard. I ran to the kitchen window, saw nothing but leaves scratching along the cement of the courtyard below.

Friday, Erika was absent from school. Saturday morning I gobbled down my breakfast, trying to decide if I should go talk to her. But when I stepped outside the front door, I was just in time to see Erika wheel her bike around the side of the building—not the front—look both ways, and then ride off.

I ran downstairs to the sidewalk. When I rounded the corner, I saw her disappear far up the street, pedaling fast.

Where was she going? To visit the guy with the strange wolfhound?

She found another friend, and she won't tell us. Won't tell me.

During the next month, Tomi and Chas seemed busier than ever. Our old habit of eating lunch together every day had changed to eating together when there wasn't a film activity for Chas or extra swim practice for Tomi. Sometimes they sat with the friends they'd made in their clubs. As for Erika, instead of the two of us getting together and writing crazy stories, she always had something she said she had to do. The few times we were together, she was busy trying to catch up on her homework and talked even less than usual.

One day after school, I sat alone in my room and read over some of the stories Erika and I had written together. They were really exciting—full of adventure and magic and strange characters . . . like werewolves.

Frowning, I turned back and realized something I'd never noticed before: most of the stories during the last year or so had werewolves in them. And not always as bad guys, either.

What was going on?

The next day, while I was waiting for Erika so we could go to math class, I wrote HARMON in a disguised handwriting on a piece of blank paper and slipped it inside her locker. I kept my face cool as she opened her locker, got it out, and read it—but instead of talking, she sagged against the wall, her face almost as white as the paper.

I felt terrible. "What's wrong, Erika? Can I help?"

Once again she turned that *look* on me. "No, Alys," she whispered. "Thanks, but, um, I have to go."

And the next day she was absent.

Chas and Tomi were sitting with me at lunch.

"There's something wrong," I said to them as soon as they put their trays down. "Really wrong." And I told them the whole story— from the canine silhouette in Erika's room to the piece of paper in the locker. "Then, last night I went down to Erika's, and even her grandmother looked worried. She wouldn't let me into the apartment. Me!" I smacked my chest. "Who's only played with Erika since kindergarten. You know what I think . . ." I hesitated, feeling really stupid.

They both looked back at me. Chas's freckled face, usually so cheerful, looked concerned. Tomi bit her lip, her dark eyes worried.

So I took a deep breath and said it: "I'm afraid this guy Cameron might be evil."

"Evil," Tomi repeated, blinking. "You mean, like gangster evil?"

"Worse," I said. "Like werewolf evil."

"Werewolf?" Tomi repeated. "You really said *werewolf*? I thought you said this guy just had a big dog."

Chas grinned. "Well, my mom keeps saying that Hollywood is full of vampires, so why not?"

"This is serious," I protested, and Tomi elbowed Chas in the side.

"Oof," Chas said, his eyes crossing.

Ignoring him, Tomi looked at me with her own eyes narrowed. "Is this really about a creepy guy with crazy powers—or is this about Alys being mad that Erika's not her shadow anymore?"

"She was never my shadow!"

"Well, she always thought up the best story-games to act out," Tomi said, "but that was when you asked for them. Are you sure you aren't just mad because she's doing stuff on her own?"

"Well . . . at first that was true," I admitted. "And because I was mad, I watched. Look. She was absent yesterday—full moon. Last month, when I first noticed the weird dog I told you about, she was also missing on the full moon day. And I think it was the same in September. She *never* used to miss a day of school. Then there's how scared she was and how scared her grandmother seemed. I thought a girl with a boyfriend is supposed to be happy. She acts like someone's blackmailing her, or something. And why else would she hide out in her room on the day of a full moon?"

Chas whistled. "You've been watching too many bad movies, Alys." He leaned forward. "Look. Why don't you join the Film Club with me? Or the creative writing group."

"You guys don't believe me," I said. "You think I'm just jealous—that I want things back the way they were when we were in grammar school."

Tomi bit her lip. "I guess this sounds like too much coincidence. Like you're making up reasons to believe this Cameron guy is more than just Erika's new friend. If you could prove anything . . ."

"Even if you could prove something," Chas said doubtfully, "what could we do?"

"Help her."

"But she hasn't asked for our help," Tomi said.

"I thought friends were supposed to be there for each other," I said, my voice going wobbly. I grabbed my books and ran away.

They didn't stop me.

That conversation kept running through my mind all afternoon. When I got home from school, I decided it was time to find Erika and *make* her talk to me. I mean, what if she *was* in real trouble? So I stashed my books and ran down to her apartment. She was coming out the front door, wearing a rain jacket and carrying her school backpack. She stopped when she saw me. She didn't look overjoyed.

I'd been planning to say, *We've got to talk.* What I actually said was, "Uh, going somewhere? I thought you were sick."

She shrugged. "I'm better now. Just have a few errands. Rain's coming," she added, looking at the sky. "I guess I'd better get moving."

I squinted up at the patch of steel-gray sky just visible beyond the upper story, then looked down in time to see her sneak a quick peek at me.

I should have spoken my piece, but instead I wimped out again. Maybe she was fine after all and was just sick of me. "Well, if you're busy, I guess I'll be going. If you want to come by later to get the homework assignment for math, you can, you know."

She gave me a grin of sheer relief. "Yeah, well, catch you later, Alys. Thanks for coming by." Now that I was leaving, she sounded a lot friendlier.

I walked slowly toward the stairs again, but as soon as I was around the corner, I bolted upstairs, grabbed my jacket and the spray can of Mace my dad had given me for emergencies, and then ran down and got my bike. Five minutes later, I spotted her battered old Schwinn flashing between the palm trees along our street. She rode fast—faster than I would have thought Erika could—and never once looked back.

Cutting through the mini-mall parking lot on her trail, I stayed far enough behind that she couldn't hear my bike. A cold wind numbed my ears and fingers. Chilly fog drifted down, almost obscuring Erika's dark head.

When she neared Los Feliz, I pedaled faster. There was more traffic now, the cars hissing back and forth on the wet street.

She sailed right on past the big boulevard— and I nearly got caught by a red light. Despite the cars, she pedaled faster and so did I. We raced through the industrial section of town, until she made a turn toward an old, rundown-looking grocery store.

My glasses fogged as I bumped across the tracks. When I looked up, I couldn't see her.

Panic! I pushed my speed and just glimpsed her turning up an old, cracked street behind the grocery store. Grungy buildings flashed by.

I stopped at an alley, panting hard, and wiped my glasses before peering into the gloom. Erika was nowhere in sight. A gang of tough-looking kids across the street eyed me, so I kept going up the alley.

I almost missed her bike leaning against a tumbledown shed behind a scraggly bush. The shed stood next to an abandoned warehouse. Broken windows lined the lower floors. Trash nearly covered the weed-choked driveway.

I parked my bike next to the shed, around the corner from Erika's. Then I started poking around.

She wasn't in the shed. Rusted machinery was piled right up to the open door. I picked my way toward the building, my heart hammering somewhere in my throat, and not because I'd just ridden a couple million miles at mach speed.

I heard voices. A high, light voice—Erika. And a lower, male one, the same compelling voice I'd heard that night, but kind of raspy now.

Stopping under one of the broken windows, I strained to hear.

"...I think this stuff is pretty gross," Erika was saying.

"You're not the only one." The boy gave a hoarse chuckle.

I grabbed the splintering windowsill and pulled myself up slowly.

"Have you seen or heard anything of *them*?" he went on.

"No. And if they come around, I'll be able to smell 'em out," Erika said.

Them? Does she mean Tomi, Chas, and me? I eased up the last few inches and sneaked a peek inside the building. Saw nothing but darkness.

"I guess that's it. My grandmother's shift at the diner ends soon, and the sun's just setting. I'd better get back," Erika said. "The streets are getting more unsafe by the minute."

"You haven't told anyone anything?"

"No one," Erika said. "No one knows I'm here."

I didn't wait to hear his reply. *Them.* Feeling like the world had cracked apart, I retreated and stood for a time in the street looking around. The rain puddles threw back reflections of the streetlights, looking like gates to another world.

The moon was a huge, round, ice-pale disk,

hanging between ragged clouds. As I looked up at it, I saw five winged creatures cross it in silhouette, banking and turning together, before they dove down over the rooftops. Large birds? *Really* large birds. They made me shiver—and when I thought of small, scared Erika riding home alone, I decided to go back and face her.

I'd just walk into that warehouse and say, "Erika, since I still value our friendship, I'll ride home with you." Cool as ice.

Making my way back to the warehouse, I saw a faint light in the same window I'd been looking in before, and snuck up to it.

Erika perched on a rusty piece of machinery, facing a tall, thin guy a few years older than us. Unkempt dark hair straggled down past his collar, and his bones made sharp edges in a dirty white shirt and old jeans. Between Erika and the guy three or four little stubs of candles flickered on an upended box. By their wavering light I saw the guy's thin fingers flexing nervously.

"It'll be back in a minute," he muttered, looking intently at the ground. "I appreciate all that meat you've been bringing, but I really need something live."

"Want me to catch it before I go?" Erika offered. "Or I'll go find you another. There are a few hours of my time left—I can do my Change in a sec."

"No, what I want is for you to get out of here," the guy said. "*They* are somewhere near. I can feel it. He's got two new candidates, and he'll break them in by sending them after me. I don't want you caught by them."

"But you can't take on five slimeballs, Cameron. You can't even take on one, not the way you are," Erika protested. "We've *got* to get you some help."

The guy smiled. "You've already saved my life once, and you certainly don't owe me—" He stopped, head canting sharply up.

For a moment I caught the twin gleams of candle flames in his green eyes. Suddenly he lunged at a jumble of engine parts in a shadowy corner.

"Gotcha!" he cried, as his hands came up with a large, wildly struggling rat. He raised it, bent his head in a sudden, fierce movement, and bit it in the neck.

The rat squealed, then sagged in his hands. The guy's mouth stayed buried in the creature's filthy fur as he sucked.

I felt like ralphing. *This Cameron guy is a vampire,* I realized.

Vampires? So there really *were* vampires in stupid old traffic-filled, diet-crazy L.A.? But that thought didn't scare me as much as the next one: *Then where is the werewolf?*

Erika sat there, her shoulders hunched, watching unhappily. *She's his prisoner!* My little speech went right out of my brain, along with my anger. *I've got to help her!*

I stumbled around the side of the building, slammed open the door, and raised my Mace.

Erika and the guy stared at me in shock. I opened my mouth to speak. Then they looked past me—and someone clouted me across the back of my neck. My glasses went flying. Coarse laughter echoed hazily as I was dragged a few feet into the warehouse. I struggled, dizzy and half blind.

Cameron looked past me, his eyes glowing. "Harmon," he snarled.

Then the room exploded. Fists and noise and trash flew everywhere. A heavy body collided with me and my can of Mace zoomed off into the darkness, along with my flashlight. I fumbled backward, trying to find my glasses. A moment later a glimmer of weak light on someone else's lenses caught the edge of my vision, and a small hand thrust a familiar shape into my fingers.

"There. Now, get out of here, Alys. *Fast!*" Erika whispered urgently. "You're in danger here."

I jammed my glasses on my face in time

to see Cameron knee one creep and duck a punch from another. He seemed to know something about street fighting, but he was slow, and his punches lacked force. It was clear he was about to get the worst of it; Erika had noticed, as well, for she dove into the battle, picking up a pile of iron gears and flinging them at the two guys cornering her vampire friend. A thin girl in punk clothes, with glowing green eyes, jumped Erika from behind. They crashed down, then another of the black-clad punks pinned Erika to the ground. A moment later, the first two got the drop on Erika's skinny vampire friend.

"Here. Let's have some fun," the guy sitting on Erika snarled—with some difficulty, as she was squirming pretty violently.

A new voice—a soft, suave voice I'll never forget—spoke next. "Yes. Let's," was all it said. But the words seemed to come straight from one of the hotter precincts of Hell. Looking up, I saw a tall man dressed entirely in black. He had a sharp-boned face, his skin nastily pale in the wildly flickering candlelight. He ignored everyone but Erika's vampire, fixing him with a deadly smile as though they two were alone. "It's been an interesting chase, Cameron," this new guy said.

"Let me go, Harmon!" cried the vampire boy. He began struggling wildly against the two creeps holding him. They were both teenaged but as pale as Harmon. The guys holding Erika down didn't look as creepy as the vampires, but they sure acted like creeps as they laughed maliciously.

"You two are only half immortal," Harmon said to them. "It is time to join us." Smiling cruelly, the man pointed at Erika. "Make your first feast now, while Cameron watches."

Erika gave a marrow-chilling yowl and lunged with tremendous strength. With a weird ripple her body changed shape. The guy sitting on her fell off, squawking, and Erika flung herself at Harmon. Wiry hair was sprouting along her arms and neck. Fantastic shadows merged and broke in the fitful candlelight, and then I could see the wolf as clearly as anything.

Erika. *The werewolf was Erika.* I couldn't move. *My best friend has just changed into a werewolf!*

The followers sprang to defend their boss. One blundered into the box with the candles.

When flames began licking redly along the spilled trash on the ground, I saw a horrifying sight: Cameron leaning over one of Harmon's vampire candidates, his mouth on the creep's neck. The guy's upturned face stared at the shadowy ceiling, death-pale and caught forever in an expression of angry surprise.

Then Cameron stood, his green eyes glowing with power. He stretched out his arms, his fingers spread and almost radiating electricity.

The man in black slowly clapped his hands. "Ah, Cameron, it's about time, don't you think? That one was weak, but now *you* are strong." His soft voice went even chillier when he laughed. "And it was good, wasn't it? Now it's time to come back to us—"

Instead, Cameron flung off the vampire kid trying to grab him, this time almost effortlessly. Harmon made a slight gesture. The two vampire kids closed in on Cameron again, looking determined. Harmon sauntered forward, pulling out a steel knife.

And he headed right for the wolf—for Erika.

I looked around frantically, wondering what I could grab to fend the guy off with, and then I heard a familiar voice, accompanied by a very strong strong smell that reminded me of spaghetti and ravioli.

"Alys? Is Erika with you—yipes!"

Chas barged in, clutching a bulging shopping bag, and then stopped dead. Tomi almost smashed into him, a fork and knife gripped in either hand.

"She was right," Chas yelled. "There really *is* a werewolf!" And he ripped apart his bag and yanked out a handful of pale, lumpy necklaces.

"Watch out! Vampires," I screamed, pointing at Harmon and his friends.

"Vam—" Tomi started nervously.

"—*pires?*" Chas squeaked. He shook his head and then turned and threw one of his wreaths over the vampire kid closest to him. The vampire clutched at the wreath and screamed.

Tomi dashed forward, brandishing the silverware at everyone. The vampires ran this way and that, ducking and waving their arms to avoid the pale, smelly wreaths Chas held in front of himself. Tomi lunged at the werewolf, who backed away with whimpers of fear and pain.

The vampire kids stumbled out of the warehouse. Chas advanced slowly on Harmon, a necklace held in each hand. Tomi closed in on the other side, waving her mother's best silver. The tall vampire backed off a step, his fangs bared. Then he flickered and turned into a huge bat. For a moment he hung above us, wings beating. Erika, a wolf in tattered kid's clothing, lunged upward. Her teeth snapped not far from the long bat wings.

With a squeak of anger, the bat wheeled toward the door, where his followers crowded, yelling threats at us. Erika moved forward, wolf teeth bared. Chas threw more wreaths, which the vampire kids dodged. Yelping and cursing, they ran off into the darkness.

"We better get outta here," I shouted, my voice shaking.

"Wait, there's still the werewolf!" Chas

headed toward Erika as he brandished one of
his stinky necklaces. "And another vampire!"
he added, spotting Cameron in the far corner.

"The wolf is Erika," I yelled, and then I
recognized the necklaces. "Garlic wreaths!"

"For werewolves," Chas said, looking
around and blinking in puzzlement. "Wait, I
don't get it. Who's *he?*" He pointed at Cameron, who edged away from the garlic wreaths
swinging from Chas's hands.

Erika was cringing away from Tomi and
her silverware. "Uh, Tomi," I said. "Can you
put your silver away? I think it's hurting
Erika."

"Erika?" Tomi said. She shoved the silverware into her coat pocket. She frowned at the
wolf. "Is that *really* her?"

"Erika?" Chas exclaimed. "What'd they *do*
to you?"

"Can you change back?" I asked.

The wolf shook its muzzle, and then its
head drooped, reminding me suddenly of Erika's shy hunching. Crazy as it sounds, for a
moment I wanted to laugh.

"Her clothes are ruined," Cameron said.

Erika nosed at her backpack.

"Is there a change of clothes in there?" I said.

The muzzle went up and down this time.
She snatched the backpack in her jaws and disappeared into the back of the warehouse.

"Let's get going," Cameron said, "before the effect of the garlic wears off, and they come back."

The three of us started toward the door. I couldn't think of anything to say—my mind was numb.

A moment later there was Erika, her normal, skinny little self. Shrugging into her backpack, she led the way outside.

Our bikes were still leaning, unmolested, against the shed. As Erika got on hers, Cameron turned into a bat.

Tomi gave him a wide-eyed look, and then we raced down the alley.

We stopped behind some bushes near the school parking lot. Erika's eyes were constantly searching the sky.

"I think we've lost them," she said at last.

Cameron drifted down, his bat shape rippled into a shadow that lengthened and hardened into human form. "Those garlic wreaths probably made them pretty sick," he said. He still radiated that powerful new energy. "Erika, I thank you for your help. But this is not what I wanted to happen. I'd better go."

Erika opened her mouth to protest.

"I owe you one," Cameron said, making a gesture to silence her. "And someday I'll be back to pay up. But first I've got to find a way out of this curse—and to stay clear of Harmon and his followers. If I'm gone, they won't be able to find you again. You or your friends."

He gave us all a brief smile that didn't reach those eerie green eyes. Then he turned and walked away. A moment later we saw a bat cruise low over the roof of the familiar school buildings.

We turned back to Erika, whose face was pale and serious in the moonlight. She wasn't hunched over, though, or scared looking as she faced us.

"Silverware *and* garlic?" I said, before anyone could speak.

Chas shrugged, his usual grin a little crooked. "So I watch too many crummy movies, too." Then he turned toward Erika and was serious. "Alys followed you. Tomi and I knew there was a problem, but at first we didn't believe Alys."

"Until I got home from school—Chas was with me—and my mom asked us how long the house guests were staying at Erika's grandmother's."

"House guests?" I said, confused.

"She must have seen my granny buying the meat I took every other day to Cam," Erika said.

Tomi nodded. "That's exactly what happened. But Chas and I wondered if it was related to this giant dog Alys had seen last month—a spooky giant dog that she thought was a werewolf."

"We kinda believed it and kinda didn't," Chas said. "So we figured it was time to investigate. Find out if there really *was* a werewolf and if it, or he, was blackmailing you for food or else he'd munch you. Or something . . ." Chas waved his hand uncertainly.

"So when we saw you leave, and Alys blasting along right behind you, I grabbed some silver for just in case and we followed *her*," Tomi put in. "But when we got to the warehouse, Chas insisted we had to go back to that yucky-looking store and get that stupid garlic." Tomi sighed. "Everyone there laughed at us."

"Those old films. Sometimes it's silver, and sometimes garlic." Chas grinned. "I couldn't remember if silver was for vampires and garlic for werewolves, or the other way around."

"I've seen it both ways," I said.

Chas scratched his head and grinned. "I guess the directors couldn't find a vampire or a werewolf to check their facts."

"So anyway," Tomi said, "we thought we'd better bring both." She finished briskly, sounding as though all this was completely normal. Except she was shivering—and nobody was fooled.

"All right. Now you know about me,"

Erika said, starting to hunch up again. "What're you going to do?"

"Nothing," I said. "Why couldn't you tell us?" My glasses fogged with tears. "Why couldn't you tell *me*?"

She rubbed her hands up her arms. "You don't like people being different, Alys. I mean, from when we were little. People change. Sometimes you can't help it."

"What happened?" Tomi asked. "Does your grandmother know?"

"Yeah, she does," Erika said. "She's one, too."

"Your granny?" I cried in disbelief.

"Yes, we've even gone out together. But since she's older, her powers don't last as long as mine do. It's an old curse, hits every other generation. Maybe it's one of the reasons why my parents wouldn't keep me. Gran told me on my last birthday. Said if it was going to happen, it would be this year."

"I take it this is not something you cure with antibiotics and vitamin C," Chas joked.

Pretty lame, but Erika gave a faint smile as she shook her head.

No one spoke for a minute. I looked up at the coldly gleaming stars, so familiar, above the familiar city. I felt weirder than ever.

Chas cleared his throat. "Where'd you find that Cameron guy?"

Head bent, Erika spoke in a low voice. "I

met him two months ago, when I was out roaming around in my wolf form. I could sense someone . . . *different*. Being a werewolf isn't just having a wolf's senses. You can sense other things. Creatures of the night. So I found Cam. He was awfully sick, and on the run. But he trusted me. He'd run away from a horrible foster home, and this guy, this Harmon, met him on a street and offered him a place to stay. Cam went to sleep and when he woke up, it was to find two fast-healing marks on his neck and this guy telling him he was now half-vampire. Seems that Harmon's got this great idea to build up an army of vampire kids, and . . . I don't know. I didn't want the details."

"Yuck," Tomi exclaimed softly.

"Well, Cam doesn't want to suck people's blood," Erika went on. "He fought it—and kept getting sicker and sicker—and finally ran away. He's trying to find a cure. I hope he can. There's no cure for me, not until you can change your genes, but I've gotten used to it— I don't have to kill people to live. Anyway, I helped him by getting rats and stuff for him. Pretty gross . . . but the alternative is much grosser. So I just had to try to help him."

"That's as good a cause as any," Tomi said. "But we would have believed you. We would have helped."

"Think about it," Erika said, straightening

up. Her eyes glowed reddish behind her glasses. "You wake up one night, and you're a werewolf. You're weird, really *weird*, for the rest of your life. In the past, former friends used to chase my family with pitchforks and torches when they found out."

"But we're *us*." Chas moved suddenly, giving Erika a quick hug. "And you're *you*. Aw, c'mon, Erika, what's a little fur among friends?"

Tomi looked from Chas to Erika to me and then said, "We'll deal with this. And we won't blab."

"So how about if we talk this over tomorrow, somewhere nice and warm. I'm freezing, and if we don't get home soon, we'll all be in bigger trouble than Harmon tried to land us in," Chas finished.

We went back to our bikes. Erika checked the sky, sniffing at the cold air. "They're gone," she said.

We began rolling slowly homeward. Tomi and Chas pulled ahead, talking back and forth, and before long I heard Chas's familiar snicker. "Vampires. Werewolves. Whoa," he muttered, and I knew that by tomorrow he'd be trying to work out a film idea using Erika's talents.

Erika rode next to me, silent for a long time.

When she spoke again, she sounded a little like her old self, though she was no longer hunching down. She hadn't gotten any taller or bigger, but somehow she seemed strong. I had a feeling she would never be my shadow again.

"You know," she said, "if you keep hanging around me, you'll have to park your silver ring. And those old earrings of your grandmother's."

"I always thought silver was kind of boring," I said. And then I took a chance. "Okay, I guess I've been judging people—I guess I just miss the old days, when we were kids. When it was just the four of us. So you changed outside, but I can change inside. We can be friends in a new way. You can trust me," I said.

She shrugged sharply, then turned around at last, her eyes glowing still. "Does that trust go two ways?"

"Always," I said.

She swiped a hand across her eyes, dashed away a glitter.

"See you tomorrow," she said.

Sure it's a tomb. Sure it's ancient.
Why would that make you think everything
inside is dead?

THE SIGHT OF THE BASILISK

Lois Tilton

The sound of a footstep. The faintest echo from
the upper level of the tunnels.
    Go away. Death waits here in the tomb.
The footsteps were light. They hesitated.
    I am the basilisk. The sight of me is death.
Another pause. Another cautious step, so
light that only the most sensitive ear could
have sensed the intruder's presence.
    Go away. I am the guardian of the tomb.
I am death.

For over a thousand years, the basilisk had
guarded the tomb where an ancient king lay buried. Tunnels of stone led down to the innermost
chamber, and there was piled a treasure, the
wealth of a kingdom: high crowns and gleaming

rings, all gold and set with brilliant jewels. There were ornaments of carved ivory and jade, of lapis and ruby. There were jars of sweet incense and bitter myrrh. And there was the sarcophagus itself: the outer coffin of precious, aromatic cedar, the inner coffin of solid gold.

The tomb was a labyrinth of stone hidden beneath the desert, tunnels that led down into the chill darkness where the king had lain buried for centuries. Then, many years ago, the shifting sands had left the secret entrance exposed, and grave robbers had come, drawn by legends of the treasures buried with the royalty of ancient times. The robbers had come down into the tomb, bearing torches to light their way through the dark passages, but none had ever returned.

The basilisk had been waiting there, and the sight of it was death.

The basilisk had never known the light. After a thousand years in the darkness of the tomb, it was white, except for the flaring crest behind its head, which was crimson and bore the mark of a crown. For despite its small size, it was the king of all serpents, and the most deadly. In the desert outside, at the entrance to the tomb, the white-hot sun made the air shimmer with heat, but the domain of the basilisk was silent and dark and chill.

And now there was the sound of footsteps

again in the upper passages, a new intruder in the tomb. The basilisk waited. It was death.

The intruder hesitated. The hollow echo of his footsteps in the tunnel made him shiver.

After a few moments, a coarse voice shouted from above, "Go on, you! Get down there! And don't come back until you have something to show us!"

The intruder flinched, then he took another step into the echoing emptiness. He was bone-thin, small for his age, and he was shivering not only from fear but from the cold that breathed out from the stone walls of the tunnel. His black hair was tangled, fallen into his eyes. A bruise swelled on one side of his thin face, and more welts and bruises showed where his ragged shirt was torn, where his new owners had beaten him to force him to go down into the tomb.

He had been a slave or a beggar all his short life, holding out his bowl in the hot, dusty turmoil of the camel market and crying out to the merciful for whatever small coin they could spare. His name was Sosi. If he had ever had any parents he could no longer remember them, but had gone from one master to another, each no worse than the last, and no better.

His new masters had hard hands and smelled

of sour wine. There were two of them, and they had brought him out here into the desert, a journey of three days from the city where he had been born, to this solitary place where the wind blew the sand up into his face and moaned at night, as if uneasy ghosts rode the air.

They had dug away the sand that had drifted over the hidden entrance of the tunnel, and then they forced him down into it with blows. They were grave robbers, Sosi realized then, and he was afraid, for this tomb must be guarded by some vengeful spirit if they were afraid to go down into its darkness themselves. He had heard the tales of ghosts that haunted these old burial places and of the curses that fell on those who dared to loot the treasures of the ancient kings.

Now he was shivering with dread, but he had learned years ago that there was no use in crying, no comfort. And his masters would only beat him again if he came back without the treasure. So he groped his way downward through the passage, farther and farther from the distant light and warmth of the living world above, deeper into the domain of death.

The basilisk scurried toward the sound of footsteps in the upper tunnels. Its head was held erect, and its crest was flared wide with alarm. Its forked tongue flickered, tasting the faint scent of fear in the air. It could sense even the slightest movements: the scrabbling claws of the warm furry beasts on which it fed, and the almost inaudible scritching of the beetles that lived in the cracks of the stone.

And here and there in the passages were the remains of previous grave robbers who had seen the basilisk—dry, white bones and skulls that stared dark-eyed at the basilisk as it passed: the last sight their eyes had ever seen in life.

It had been hatched in these very tunnels a thousand years ago. Soldiers of the dying king had searched the desert to discover the basilisk's nest and bring its egg, with the unborn serpent already stirring within, to the innermost chamber of the king's tomb. There the basilisk had hatched and remained to protect the treasures of his grave, awaiting the day when the hidden entrance might be exposed. All its life it had known nothing but the chill and the dark, and death.

Now it listened to the footsteps of yet another intruder, who would soon die like the rest. *Go away*, it hissed softly. *Go away. The basilisk guards this tomb.*

Sosi had gone a long way down through the tunnel. The air smelled dry and very old. If he stopped and held his breath, he could sometimes hear a faint distant scritching sound that made him think of rats in the walls of a house. A while ago he had stepped on something that snapped under his foot, and as he bent down, his sensitive fingers had discovered the shapes of tiny bones.

Now he stumbled over something larger, something that rolled away with a clattering sound. He knelt, and his hand touched the unmistakable shape of a human skull.

He dropped it with a sharp gasp of horror and heard the brittle bone crack as it struck the stone. Hot tears ran down his face, for it was clear now that his masters had sent him to his doom. Death dwelled in this tomb, guarding the ancient treasures they had sent him to steal. He could hear it approaching him now.

In terror, he dropped to his knees and held his breath. Yes, the sound was faint, but somewhere in the tunnels something was moving, the soft rasp of scales against the stone, its echo a whisper in the dark. Death, coming for him, coming closer now.

His heartbeat sounded in his ears like a drum in the silence of the tomb. He did not dare to breathe.

The basilisk was puzzled. Here he had found the intruder in the tomb, but this one was different. This grave robber bore no torch

to light his way through the darkness of the tunnels. Cautiously, the basilisk came closer until it could clearly make out the human form, crouched, kneeling on the stone floor of the passage, silent and motionless with fear. This one was much smaller than the others had been, and ragged and thin, and the scent of his terror filled the air.

The basilisk hesitated. There was something wrong. The intruder still breathed. He still lived. No creature could lay eyes on the basilisk and live, but this boy did. The basilisk could sense the rapid pulse of his heartbeat, the warmth of his body.

You do not die, it hissed softly. *Why? I am the basilisk. To look upon me is death.*

Sosi gasped aloud in shock to hear it speak. The basilisk was so close that he could have reached out and touched it. He stammered, "I . . . don't see you. I cannot see."

The tomb is dark. You carry no torch. You cannot see me in the dark?

"I see nothing. I am blind. I was blind when I was born."

The basilisk came even closer. Its forked tongue flicked out to the bare skin of the boy's arm. Sosi flinched, but otherwise held still.

You are warm, said the basilisk.

Sosi's voice shook. "Are you going to kill me now?"

Lois Tilton

The basilisk hesitated. *I guard the treasures of the king's tomb. Grave robbers must die.*

"I don't want to be a grave robber!" Sosi cried. "My masters bought me in the marketplace—they knew the darkness wouldn't matter to a blind boy. They beat me. They made me come down into the tomb. They were afraid to come themselves."

The basilisk's tongue flicked out again to the tears on the boy's face. They tasted of salt, and they were warm.

Then, cautiously, Sosi reached out a hand and stroked the length of the basilisk's body. "You are a serpent," he said in wonder. "There are serpents in the marketplace where I was born. Their masters play flutes and charm them to dance. But they were warm, and you are cold." Yet he knew that the creature before him was far, far more than any common snake charmer's pet. He alone had met the basilisk, and survived!

The basilisk sighed, a soft hiss of longing. *It is always cold in the tomb. I have felt the warmth, sometimes, from the entrance, when the wind blows away the sand. But the sun is so fierce, so hot and bright. It would burn me, and I would not be able to see.*

"You want to leave this place? I could hide you from the sun under my shirt," Sosi offered.

122

"If you didn't kill me, I could carry you out of here."

Once again, the basilisk's tongue felt the warmth of the boy's skin. The king's treasure was cold, and had lain untouched for a thousand years, a thousand years in the dark since the day the basilisk was hatched. Yet something within the serpent remembered the heat of the desert sands where its egg had lain before the king's soldiers took it from its nest. So long, so very long it had been alone and cold.

I would like to feel the warmth of the sun. Slowly, it wrapped itself around Sosi's waist, under the rags of his shirt, relaxing as it felt the heat of his body. Then they made their way back up through the tunnels, back to the entrance of the tomb, where the sun shone hot and bright.

The grave robbers seized their blind slave as soon as they saw him climb up out of the darkness of the tomb. "Where is it? Do you have the treasure? What did you bring back? Gold? Jewels?" they demanded harshly.

"I brought back death," Sosi told them, as the king of all serpents lifted its crimson-crested head from within his shirt.

And the grave robbers looked upon the basilisk.

Great gifts can sometimes bring great pain....

THE TEACHER WHO COULD HEAR

Paula McConnell

Miss Mary Stevens.

Miss Stevens, to her students—Mary, to anyone else—was a quiet, harmless teacher with an unusual ability.

She could hear.

It wasn't with her ears this remarkable gift rested, it was with her heart. She could hear waves crash on the far shore, she could hear the sound of tears sliding down young cheeks. She could hear callings most couldn't, and she could reply.

What Mary couldn't do was understand her unique gift or understand how it could possibly make her special.

Mary once heard an earthquake two thousand miles away. She heard the wooden beams crack to cover the shrieks of those who were still caught inside; she heard the lights go out in the mighty city after the tremors.

All of this Mary heard, and much more over the years.

By the time Mary attended teacher's college, she was convinced this hearing business was too risky to talk about. She had never mentioned to her aging parents that she had heard their time was due. She had never mentioned that the plans they had made for her were pointless and a waste, that she would never see her precious teacher's retirement.

She was a good girl and would do what they wished.

It became very difficult to tell her friends what she knew. Once Mary could not tell a friend she had heard her death. Elaine, a fellow teacher, had stood with Mary at the bus stop chatting away when Mary received the familiar jolt. She heard her friend's demise, and she didn't know why she was frightened, but the friend now climbing the bus stairs would soon be gone. She never told her.

Then, one night three years later, Elaine disappeared.

Over the years Mary became more afraid to hear. She drifted away from friends after the disappearance of Elaine; she never called her relatives after the passing of her parents. Eventually, no one questioned the solitude of the quiet teacher.

No one questioned her, that is, until she heard a book.

The book, *Our Sixth Grade Teacher Is Missing*, was on the desk of one of her students. It was very popular in her classroom, this copy dog-eared and worn. Many of the other teachers were heard in the teachers' lounge condemning this particular writer, calling him a reprobate and irresponsible because he killed off teachers in his stories. Miss Stevens didn't listen. She didn't believe that the other teachers, or the writer, could mean such nonsense.

Miss Stevens had pushed aside Tuesday's spelling papers to reach for the book when she heard the jolt.

Alone in the classroom, she grabbed the book and staggered to the middle of the room. Pulses of energy surged up her arm until they exploded in the center of her chest.

The book screamed, "Help me, help me!" until she could bear it no longer and dropped it and herself to the floor.

The book lay whimpering beside her.

Miss Stevens looked at it through the hair that had fallen over her face, wondering how a book could send such a message. Afraid to touch it again, she grabbed a pencil from under a desk and poked the book.

It let out a great sigh and was silent.

Did I kill it? she wondered.

Her monogrammed tote bag was nearby on her desk. She placed it on the floor and with the pencil pushed the book into the bag, being very careful not to touch it.

It went home with her that very night. It would not leave her mind. The voice was eerily familiar.

The book stayed in the bag until Friday. Mary waited until after her supper to examine it. She had borrowed another copy from the library and read it from cover to cover. It didn't speak to her. She could not find anything that unusual about it: any sixth grader could have read this book without much difficulty. She thought it sufficiently twisted to satisfy a child, but she preferred to be scared a little bit more. The author was familiar to her only through her students, and she was surprised to find he lived in her city. She looked at the tote bag.

Perhaps it won't talk to me again, Mary thought.

Her unique ability had turned itself off after the event in the classroom; she hadn't heard anyone, or anything, call her since then.

Mary opened the tote bag, reached her hand inside, and felt not only the book but a warm, sticky substance. She pulled her arm out slowly, exposing her hand and the book—both covered with blood. Horrified, Mary tried to drop the book, but it would not leave her hand; it was part of her and, worse, it was still calling.

Fear crept through her when she recognized the voice.

"Help me, help me!" It spoke directly into her mind, where the other calls had gone.

"I can't help you—I don't know how," she whispered.

"Why didn't you tell me?" the voice demanded.

The old clock left by Mary's dead parents ticked loudly on the wall. The fear in Mary intensified. It couldn't be possible that this was her friend who had been gone for three years now. The book stared at her. The ticking grew louder.

Mary took a deep breath and said, "Elaine, is that you? I couldn't . . ."

"Answer with your mind!" it said. "I will tell you how you can help me now. You can release me, Mary. Call him."

She was afraid to ask Elaine exactly where she was. Mary walked carefully to the phone table; the sight of blood made her terribly nauseated. She stopped.

"Elaine, I don't understand. Who am I calling—?"

The book slammed her arm onto the table. Mary sat slowly in the chair, looking at the blood-smeared name over the picture.

"Yes, Mary. Him."

In disbelief, she looked up the number and dialed.

"The number you have reached has been disconnected."

"The number doesn't work any longer. I can't call," she said, reeling at the sight of the bloody book still in her hand.

"Wait," the book said. "I forgot the number had changed. Use this number."

It was just like Elaine to forget a phone number at a time like this, Mary thought to herself. She dialed again. This time the phone clicked when there should have been an answer, but it wasn't a voice she could hear with her ears. She heard it in her mind.

"There is a black car waiting for you outside." *Click.*

Mary stood up from the table and somehow made it downstairs from her apartment. She heard her clock ticking. It was no longer on her kitchen wall but *inside her mind.* She heard the pages of a book. She heard laughter. Mary heard her own death.

She saw the car and turned to run, but the book groaned and pulled her into it. Inside the car she stared at the book still stuck in her hand, her chest heaving with fright.

"Mary, you *do* want to help me, don't you? After all, you could have prevented this."

Mary did not answer. Minutes, or maybe even hours, went by; she didn't have a watch and could not hear time any longer. The car stopped in what looked like a carport. The book's pages fluttered in a cool breeze Mary hadn't noticed before.

"Go inside."

Miss Mary Stevens did so.

Either the room was very dark or her eyes were failing; she could not tell. She focused on my figure. The book spoke.

"I have brought her."

Gently I took the book from Miss Stevens's hand. There was an exhausted moan as I placed the book in the bookcase with the other tattered, bloodstained paperbacks. I turned to Miss Stevens.

Shaking, she suddenly understood.

"You wrote this book! Did you kill . . . Elaine?" She looked at the paperbacks. Then

she looked at me. "And the other teachers?" she whispered.

I smiled. I walked toward her.

"My dear, such harsh words. I thought you would be honored to live in the pages of a good book. Your students will love you."

Mary could hear no longer.

Many are questioning what happened to Miss Mary Stevens, the quiet teacher. The memorial built by her students was finished in the same month my new book, *The Teacher Who Could Hear*, was released. There is a new teacher in Miss Stevens's room now. She can see things that aren't really there. She has often thought she has seen Miss Stevens reading my new release. Of course, she doesn't talk about this.

Sadly, teachers come and go. But literature always remains.

Ah, dear reader, I'm sure something like this could never happen in your tidy little room!

LIFE WITH A SLOB

Gordon Van Gelder

I first noticed it while they were fighting.

"Bob, this room is revolting!" Mom shouted. "You have absolutely no sense of responsibility at all."

"Mom, it's *my* room and I'll do whatever I want to!" Bob shouted back.

Meanwhile, the room was moving.

Not the walls and everything, of course, but the mess on the floor was moving. The millions of papers, Bob's T-shirts, his socks, all the bottles and canisters of chemicals from the week he decided to be a photographer, underwear, hamster litter (from the Great Gerbil Fiasco, when Bob's science project died on him—Bob can be so weird about animals), newspaper clippings, index cards, computer disks, and CD cases: they all scurried like ants when you lift a rock and find them underneath, only much slower. Books and papers slid under his bureau, behind the shelves, and under the night table.

"Why do we have to go through this nonsense every week?" Mom complained.

"Why don't you quit yelling at me?"

"I'm not yelling. It's not right to live this way. It isn't healthy and I don't like it."

I didn't believe what I saw. But then I heard the mess thinking, a million voices that spoke all at once, like the kids in the auditorium during a school assembly. They said things like, "Get off me, you lousy slob!" and "Maybe I can be alone if I go behind the bureau," and "Will I ever get washed?" and "The floor is so cold."

"Andy, listen to me!" my mother demanded.

I said, "Huh?"

"I asked if the room bothered you, Andy. You have to put up with Bob's mess more than I do. You have to *live* in it."

"Uh, no, Mom, I don't mind it." I knew from experience that would stop the yelling.

"You see? I told you so," Bob said.

"It's not right to live like that . . . it's not human!" She shut the door. Bob whipped a sock at the wall, muttering to himself.

Sometimes I really wonder about Bob. I mean, he's a real genius and nobody ever wins an argument with him, but he can't even clean his side of the room. He always says he's got too much work to do. He's basically okay, you know, but I wish he'd stop being mean and shouting like he has been all the time lately. Dad thinks Bob's under a lot of pressure while he waits to hear from colleges, but I think it's more like he used to say when we were little— he doesn't really want to be part of our family. He used to joke around and say he was from Brainsville and we should let him go back. Mom would always tell him to stop joking like that, but now he doesn't act like he's joking at all.

A yellow flier crumpled itself into a little ball so it could fit under the heater. "It's warm in here," it said.

"What are you staring at, wimp?" Bob demanded.

"Huh? I'm just thinking."

"Well, think somewhere else. I've got a huge load of work to do." He went to his desk and shuffled papers. "What did you do with my big green book on Spinoza?"

"Nothing."

"Then where is it?"

"Is it the book you're standing on?"

I laughed when it turned out to be the one. "Shut up, jerky boy." He turned back to his desk. "Why don't you go play with a friend, if you've even got one."

"Hey! Leave me alone."

"Do the same for me."

I stalked out of the room and went downstairs to play Civilization on the computer for a couple of hours. But when Bob went over to a friend's house to practice debating, I went back to watch the mess.

It was like a big blob that rolled around and ate everything it met. The things sounded pretty stupid. All they ever talked about was how cold they were and how much they hated Bob. I couldn't blame them, when I thought about it. The floor *was* cold, and the papers didn't exactly wear down jackets.

As I watched, I noticed a funny thing. None of them would come past the dresser and onto my side of the room.

"Why won't they come over here?" I said to myself.

All of a sudden, the voices stopped and one loud voice said inside my head, *Because you don't allow dirtiness. You have to permit us to come over.*

Whoever it was, it was right. I always picked up after myself and put my games away, and I even swept when Mom asked me to. The mess couldn't possibly get onto my side of the room.

Then I wondered where all the other voices had gone.

I am all the voices, the mess said in my head. *I am the Mess.*

"Well, Mess, feel free to come onto my side of the room. I'll pick you up if you want."

No! Don't pick me up!

"Sorry. I just thought you wanted to be warm."

If you pick me up, I'll die faster than a tadpole on land.

"Well, then, how about if I throw a blanket on you?

I'd like that very much. I pulled a blanket off Bob's bunk and threw it on the Mess. I covered as much of the Mess as possible, but there was no way I could cover the whole thing.

Thank you, said the Mess.

Watching everything move around had gotten kind of boring by then, so I picked up my cyberpunk novel from underneath Bob's jacket. I could only hear the voices if I tried, so it was easy to ignore them. But it was impossible for me to stop thinking about them. Finally, I put the book down and said, "Mess? Mister Mess?"

Yes, Andy?

"Mess, why do you hate Bob? I mean, if he wasn't such a slob, you wouldn't exist."

He treats me like dirt.

"Whadda you mean?"

He steps on me, he blames everything on me, he does nothing for me. When you left the room today, he kicked me as hard as he could.

"Well, he was mad at Mom."

Exactly. So Mr. Brainiac decides to take it out on me. He takes everything out on me. You think I like it when he throws parts of me at you? My hand automatically felt the stitches I got in my ankle when Bob threw his metal coin box at me after he got a C on a physics test. *I hate him, Andy. Do you know what I'm going to do? I'm going to make his life miserable. I'll teach him to handle me with more respect. He'll learn.*

It sounded good to me, so I went back to the book. Later, when I went to sleep, I felt kind of weird, so I said, "Good night, Mess."

Good night, Andy, it said pleasantly.

Sunday afternoon, while Bob worked on his English term paper, I sat on my bed and talked with the Mess. Bob couldn't hear us, of course, so I acted like I was reading a magazine so he wouldn't think I was crazy. Bob didn't mind my being there until the Mess started making me crack up. I would have stopped, but I couldn't. The Mess was imitating Bob's gurgling laugh, the squeak in his voice when he yells, everything.

"Will you shut up, twerp!"

Will you shut up, Bob? echoed the Mess. I tried to stop laughing, but I couldn't.

"Get out of here," Bob said. "I've got a lot of work to do, and I can't waste time listening to you giggle to yourself. Why don't you go out and get a friend."

"Shut up, Bob. Leave me alone."

"Then stop laughing, you idiot."

I did. *Now do you see why I can't stand him?* Mess asked me.

"Yeah."

I doubt he likes anybody.

"He hates us, but not all the time, that's all."

Bob glared at me. "I said, get outta here, wimp."

Well, he isn't just loathsome, he's also late for work.

My clock read 3:10. "Bob, you've got to go to work."

"Shut up, dolt. I worked this morning." He dug around on his desk for his clock.

"I know. I woke you up, remember? But you have to go back and help close up the store, don't you?"

"Yeah, but I don't have to go till . . . whoa!" He raced out the door.

Not even a thank you, commented the Mess.

"He's just bad at remembering, that's all. I

mean, I guess it's a lot of responsibility putting together all the Sunday papers *and* having to close the store."

He's worse than a dustbuster.

I thought about how much that must mean to the Mess. "He's not that bad."

Really? Do you like *having to wake him up every Sunday morning at 5:45 just to get him out of bed?*

"No, not at all. Hey, how come you're so smart, Mess?"

Because I'm the cumulative intelligence of all the materials that you call the Mess. I am the intelligence in this sweaty shirt and in that crumpled piece of plastic and in these pieces of popcorn and in everything else, all mixed in one.

"Well, if you're so smart, how come you hate Bob?"

Every inch of every piece of every component of every section of me hates him more than you can understand. Watch this. In one big wave, the Mess reared up, spinning around like a small tornado, and stormed its way to the desk. It sucked up his translation for Greek class. In a second, fourteen pages of notes were ripped into a million pieces.

"He'll kill you! He spent two weeks on that stuff. You're dead meat."

I fear nothing. I hope he flunks.

"Jeez, he's going to blame me for it and take it out on me. Oh, why did you have to do that?"

If he touches you, I'll kill him.

"Okay." I looked at the pieces of Bob's assignment. "You wouldn't really kill him, would you? You know, like dead?"

I'd hurt him very badly.

"Well, don't mess him up too bad, okay? He hasn't *always* been this bad. I mean, we used to be sort of friends."

Okay, Andy.

As we talked, I noticed that some pieces of paper and an oily rag had moved under my desk.

In one week, Mess and I became good friends. On Monday I kept it from destroying Bob's computer when it found out Bob had made a back-up copy of his translations. On Wednesday I got really mad at Bob because he kept busting on me while we were doing dishes.

"Don't you have one friend?" he would say. "Just one little friend?"

No matter what I told him about Jimmy Mullins or Steven Sloan or even Wallace Nichols, though, he kept on bugging me. I finally whipped a bowl of creamed corn at him and locked myself in our room. God, I was so mad!

When I got into the room and started talking with Mess, though, I cooled off. He did Bob imitations and stuff until I felt really mellow.

Then came Sunday morning. The alarm went off by my head at 5:45, and I was going to reach up and give Bob a shove to wake him up like I always do, but Mess said, *Maybe you should try something different this fine morning, Andy?* He sounded as if he was up to something really nasty, but I was half asleep, so I didn't notice it.

BUZZ! The alarm went off again, this time in Bob's ear. He jumped up in his bunk and banged his head on the ceiling. Every one of Mess's million voices laughed.

"Andy, you're gonna get it!" He swung a fist at me, missed, and fell off the bunk and onto the Mess.

"I have you now!" Mess shouted.

Bob tried to get up, but he couldn't. Shirts and socks tied his hands and feet together. Paper clips jabbed themselves into his hands, and a pair of extension cords whipped him. Books jumped up and down on his chest and stomach, the fat books he's always studying. He tried to yell, but there were socks in his mouth.

The Mess was big but Bob was bigger. His hands broke free and tried to untie his feet, but by the time he was done, the Mess had lashed him to his desk. Bob broke free and stood up, but then he fell down with a loud thump.

He pulled a Hefty bag off his face, flopping around like a fish out of water, and shouted, "Make it stop, Andy! Make it stop!"

"Make it stop, *what?*" I asked sweetly.

"Make it stop, *please,* Andy. For God's sake, make it stop."

"Mess, stop."

But I'm just warming up. Surely you won't make me stop now, will you?

"You've done enough, Mess."

The papers fell to the floor.

Bob stood up, bleeding and angry. "I'm gonna kill you, wimp. I'm really gonna kill you."

Thump. He fell to the floor.

"What are you going to do, Bob?"

"I'm sorry. I'm sorry. Just let me go!"

"Let him go, Mess."

Bob went straight for the door. "You're gonna pay."

"Bob, aren't you late for work? Didn't your boss say that he'd fire you the next time you were late?"

"You're dead, wimp. You are dead meat." And he raced out the door.

"Good job, Mess," I said, smiling.

Any time, Andy. Any time at all.

When Bob came back from work, he didn't mention the fight. He probably thought it was a dream—Bob couldn't understand something if it wasn't scientific. All I know is that the first thing he did when he got back was clean the room until he found the floor. He cleaned everything. There wasn't a single dust bunny on the floor when he finished. The room shone like a TV commercial. He even returned the sunglasses he borrowed from me last year. When he had to go back to work, he was a whole half hour early.

But the Mess wasn't dead. He had started under my desk, and he grew quickly during the next few weeks, until my whole side of the room had wall-to-wall Mess carpeting. Bob rearranged Dad's old office and moved in, even though he would be leaving for Harvard in less than five months. And he kept the room spotless. Mom couldn't understand our sudden switch.

Now that Bob's in Cambridge, he thinks he's free. And he is—at least until he gets my package. I wish I could see his face when he gets all his old socks!

Me and my friend Mess will get a big kick out of it.

Some people just don't know when to keep their big mouths shut.

CAMPFIRE

S. Anthony Gardner

Somewhere beyond the light, crickets chirped, and other things made other noises. The sound of logs burning fought head to head with the sound of the boys' breaths rasping in suspense.

"So, the guy goes around the car to let his girl out," Charlie said, leaning toward the fire, "when alluva sudden he screams and keels over cuz hanging there on the door handle is this bloody hook!"

Charlie stared at the other boys sitting around the fire and shivered in spite of himself. Their eyes were wide, seemingly unaffected by the sharp smoke of the campfire. After half an hour of continuous shockers, the boys had become entranced with fear from their own stories.

Mr. Petersen cleared his throat. He was

watching one of the campers doodling in the dust, uninterested in "The Hook," "Chicken Heart," "The Monkey's Paw," and similar yarns the other boys were spinning. An orphan, the child had been sent to camp because his foster parents thought the company of other boys would do him good.

"Danny, do you have a story you'd like us to hear?"

"Nah, he's just a big gob of chicken doo. He's too scared to talk." This came from Brian, the bully of the group. "Nothin' he says can scare me."

Danny looked up at the circle of boys. Behind the flash of thick lenses, his eyes were focused on a place far away. He looked tired, almost old. When he spoke, his voice brought to mind dried-out branches rubbing at the window of a deserted house at midnight.

"The devil has a special name," he said. "A secret name, and if you say it out loud, he'll come and take you away."

"Says who?" cried Brian. "Where'd you hear that kind of junk?"

"He told me. The devil."

Skin crawled, mouths went dry. Some of the campers were definitely impressed.

"You're full of it. I ain't afraid to say no old name." The boys gazed from Brian to Danny, from Danny to Brian. Things could be shaping up for a fight, and for the boys that was almost as good as a ghost story. "C'mon, what's his name? I'll say it."

Danny dug in his pockets for a few moments and came up with a scrap of paper and the stub of a pencil. He frowned in concentration and then scribbled something down. The paper was folded carefully and passed to the boy on Danny's right. The grubby slip went halfway around the circle to Brian. Mr. Petersen looked on curiously.

Brian unfolded the paper and scowled at it. Then he looked at Danny and scowled at him.

"This is it? I gotta say this?"

Danny only nodded.

"This is so stupid, I'm not just gonna say it, I'm gonna yell it so everybody in four counties knows how stupid you are."

Brian stood up, arms raised to the sky. He grinned at the other boys, then took an enormous breath and screamed something so vociferously that Mr. Petersen couldn't understand him. Looking at Danny again, Brian crumpled the paper up, and threw it into the flames.

"So much for you, chicken doo. I'm gonna go water the flowers."

Mr. Petersen looked at Danny. The boys looked at Danny. Danny looked at Mr. Petersen. The man cleared his throat uncomfortably.

"Well, campers, I think that's enough for—"

From the woods to his left, where Brian had disappeared only seconds before, came a sharp cry that set the hair on Mr. Petersen's neck standing on end. It wasn't so much the sheer animal terror in the cry, he realized, but the abrupt end to it, as if the crier's throat had been crushed, or his lungs ripped from his chest.

Danny took his glasses off and began polishing them on the bottom edge of his T-shirt. His small shoulders rose and fell in a sad sort of shrug.

"My parents didn't believe me, either."

This ghost story, set in France, is haunting in the best sense of the word.

PAST SUNSET

Vivian Vande Velde

There was a street in the village where I grew up that everyone knew not to travel down past sunset.

During daylight hours, it was a perfectly fine and normal street. Housewives opened their shutters and strung clotheslines across the way so that fresh-smelling laundry hung to dry two and three and four stories above the cobblestones that the neighborhood grandfathers kept well swept. Merchants from the surrounding countryside set up stalls to sell fresh fruit and vegetables, live chickens, and rabbits. While the sun was there to warm the stones, you could hear the *clop clop* of horses' hooves and the rumble of the wooden wheels of carts and carriages. You could hear the laughter of young boys playing their chasing games and the rhythmic counting of girls playing their games of skipping and hand clapping.

But as the sun began to set, the farmers hurried to take down their stalls and return to the safety of their country homes. The housewives pulled in their sheets and shirts and locked the shutters. Those who lived on other streets of the village found different routes on their way home, and parents didn't have to call their children in, because the children knew not to linger outside.

For when the shadows blended into night's darkness, there was a lady you would see if you were foolish enough to look. Your first thought might be that she was pale and beautiful, standing there in a white gown that flowed in the evening breeze. Silently she would beckon for you to come closer. You might be fooled by her sad face. But then you might remember that there wasn't necessarily a breeze that night. And then you might notice that she was much too pale, even for a fine lady. And if you looked at her eyes . . .

Never look at her eyes, the stern grandmothers in their black shawls warned us—for there was no looking away.

The children of the village would always reach an age—for us girls it was often when we were nine or ten, for the boys, usually a year or so earlier—when all our parents' and grand-parents' and neighbors' warnings weren't enough; when, in fact, those warnings only served to stir curiosity, and stir it and stir it, until we had to see for ourselves what we had so long been warned about; when we would find a way—there was always a way—to locate our-selves in a room that overlooked the street; when we would crack open the shutters and al-ternately hope and dread that this would be one of the nights that the ghostly lady appeared.

Those nights that she *did* appear, she al-ways found the cracked-open shutter—no mat-ter how quiet the would-be observer had been and no matter that we almost always knew enough not to have a candle in there with us to show a telltale sliver of light into the street.

But she always knew.

And if there was an open window, she would come and stand directly beneath it, and—always silently—she would motion for that child to come out in the street to join her.

We might have been curious, but we weren't stupid.

If we were especially daring or if we weren't fast enough, the lady—whose feet nor-mally seemed as firmly placed on the ground as our own—would begin to drift up, up, closer and closer until we would slam the shutters closed and stand or crouch with our hearts

beating wildly to have seen that everything was exactly as it had always been described to us, and thankful that—for whatever reason—this particular ghost's domain was outside, on our street, and she couldn't pass through walls or shutters.

But there was always the fear that someday a child would be too daring or too slow.

This had never happened in recent memory. But Grandmère Edmée—who wasn't actually anybody's grandmother, but who was probably the oldest person living in the village—Grandmère Edmée remembered a ghost long before the citizens had risen up in revolution and sent the king and his family to the guillotine. Grandmère Edmée said there was a ghost when she herself was our age—a hard enough concept to believe in itself—but she added that then the ghost was a young man, not a young woman. She also said that her own grandmother talked of a ghost who was an old woman—an old woman who had been cursed by a witch. But who she was or why she had been cursed, nobody knew. This talk of ghosts who changed age and gender made *us* say that Grandmère Edmée had spent too much time in the wine cellar. But nobody wanted to see what would happen if the ghost *did* touch you, or if you looked into her eyes.

All of this—all of it—changed the autumn I was twelve.

By then I had seen the ghostly lady often enough that I was cautious—no one ever outgrew caution—but I was no longer impressed. I would have gladly given up our famous ghost to live on a normal street, like my friends who could stay out past sunset and who could leave their windows open on a hot summer's night. As my brother Antoine had done before me, I became less interested in seeing the ghost and more interested in making sure the younger members of my family took no reckless chances.

In our house, where the kitchen and the parlor looked out over the street, the adults generally spent the evening in the parlor, with the shutters closed. We were two stories up, with the patisserie selling its wonderful tarts and pies on the ground floor and the Guignard family occupying the middle floor.

One evening of the year I was twelve, when autumn teetered on the brink of winter, I was in the kitchen because my ten-year-old sister Mignon claimed to have a chill; this required sitting by the kitchen fire after the rest of the family had moved to the parlor. Our brother Gaetan, who was nine, had offered to keep her company—a clear signal, as far as I was concerned, that the kitchen shutters would bear close watching that night.

So I was embroidering a rose on a dinner napkin to cover a stain, while Gaetan whittled a piece of wood that was eventually supposed to be an extra sheep for the Christmas crèche and Mignon—sulking at being found out—was huddled close to the fire, wrapped in a blanket.

A noise at the side window made us all jerk our heads up.

It sounded like pebbles—or beans—hitting the outside of the shutters.

"Marianne," Mignon called to me in a whisper. "What was that?"

Before I could answer that I didn't know, a voice called, "Jules," which was my grandfather's name.

The voice belonged to the widow Morin, who lived next door above the butcher's shop, her kitchen window separated from ours by a very narrow alley.

Mignon, in a strong voice that belied her claims of not feeling well, called out, "Grandpère! Maman! Papa!"

Fifteen-year-old Antoine was the first into the kitchen, followed by Maman, then Honorée—who was six—and then Grandpère. Papa was last because he'd hurt his foot in an accident at the mill and still had to use a cane.

"Jules!" the widow Morin called. "Are you there? I need help."

"Open the window," Grandpère commanded us.

"No!" Maman objected. She had been born on one of the farms in the outlying district, and—even after twenty years—was still terrified of living in the village and overlooking the street. As far as I know, she had never been tempted to crack open the shutters and peek at the ghostly lady.

Papa balanced on his cane so he could pat Maman's hand. "It will be safe if we don't look down," he assured her.

It was Antoine who unfastened the shutters. Fifteen-year-old boys fear so little.

By then Grandpère had made his way around the table to the window. "Hélène," he greeted the widow. "What's the matter?"

"It's Jean-Pierre," she called, leaning out of her own kitchen window. "I dropped his medicine."

We all looked at each other. Jean-Pierre was her grandson. Although he was fully as big as Antoine, in reality he was only ten years old, and his thinking was that of a much younger child. For the past three years, the widow Morin had been giving Jean-Pierre medicine that was supposed to make him smarter, though in three years none of us had seen a change. But that wasn't the medicine she was talking about.

157

"I was going to give him a dose of the medicine for his coughing," the widow Morin explained, "and the bottle slipped out of my hand and broke."

We could hear Jean-Pierre coughing, sounding as though he'd break apart from the force of it. He'd been coughing since last winter, and with the new winter starting it had gotten worse. Jean-Pierre, who used to be so large, seemed to get thinner by the day.

The widow Morin lowered her voice, as though we across the alley could hear without her grandson hearing. "I thought maybe we could make it through one night without, but . . ." She shook her head.

"What does she expect of us?" Maman demanded, louder than was necessary if she meant the question just for us.

"Hush," Papa whispered.

"What does she expect of us?" Maman repeated.

I saw the widow Morin's frantic look.

"I'll go get more medicine for Jean-Pierre," Grandpère assured her.

"No!" Maman said.

Grandpère gave Antoine's elbow a shove, and Antoine knew enough to smile politely, then close and bolt the shutters.

"Why should you risk yourself in the night?" Maman cried.

"Because Hélène is crippled by old age," Grandpère said. "And I am not."

"Pardon me," Maman said, "but you overestimate yourself."

"Hush!" Papa said again, this time not whispering. Grandpère was his father, not Maman's.

"Maman is right," Antoine said. Papa raised his hand to cuff him, but Antoine took a step back and said, "Grandpère, you are in remarkable condition for a man of seventy years, but I can make it from our doorstep to the corner in about half a minute. I think you have to admit that it would take you considerably longer." He turned to Papa. "And you, with your cane," he continued, "would take even longer than Grandpère." To Maman he said, "Surely you're not saying that none of us should go. Surely you're not saying that we should let Jean-Pierre die."

Maman looked as though that was exactly what she wanted to say.

I thought she was a horrid person. I thought Antoine was the bravest boy I'd ever heard of.

But Maman relented. "At least wait for her," Maman suggested. "Don't go out until after she walks by. That will improve your chances that you won't meet her."

"Your mother makes sense," Papa said, though some nights the ghostly lady came very late, and other nights she did not come at all. "Open the window to watch."

So Antoine opened the shutters. "Madame Morin!" he called. "We will wait until the lady has passed. . . ."

The widow cast a worried look back into her house, in the direction from which we could hear Jean-Pierre coughing. Hesitantly, not daring to complain, she nodded her thanks.

If Gaetan and Mignon were hoping that the extraordinary circumstances would allow them to catch their first glimpses of the ghostly lady, Maman was too fast for them. She set me to helping them get ready for bed and said, "Afterwards, Marianne, you and I will sit in the parlor. We'll keep each other awake."

The reason she suggested this was that there was a window in the north wall of the parlor that also looked out over the street. Maman didn't want the younger children sneaking out of their bedrooms for a peek while we were all in the kitchen, and she didn't trust me not to do the same by myself.

So once I saw the little ones firmly, if reluctantly, settled, we sat, Maman and I in the parlor and Antoine, Papa, and Grandpère in the kitchen. The only one who showed a tendency to sleepiness was Grandpère—a room away, I could hear him snoring. Periodically, Papa's injured foot must have bothered him—for I could hear him get up and move stiffly about the kitchen. It was during one of those times that I heard him say, suddenly, sharply, "Antoine! Antoine! Move away from the window!"

I jumped to my feet and Maman was only a step behind me.

In the kitchen, Antoine was at the front window, the one that faced the street, leaning against the sill and looking out with such intensity I knew what had to be there.

Papa let his cane drop to the floor with a clatter as, dragging his foot behind, he tried to hurry across the distance that separated him from Antoine. Papa grabbed Antoine by the shoulders and hurled him away, then he slammed the shutters closed.

"Jules?" we heard the widow call across. But she must have heard the commotion. She must have known what it was about, for she didn't open her own shutters.

"It's all right," Grandpère shouted to her, looking from Papa to Antoine. From having fallen asleep with his head on the table, what he had of hair was all sticking up.

"Fool," Papa called Antoine. "*Never* look at her eyes."

"I wasn't," Antoine protested, rubbing his shoulder where it had struck against the pantry door. But his gaze strayed back to the now-barred shutters.

"Fool," Papa repeated.

"What happened?" Maman demanded.

"She was halfway up the wall," Papa said.

"She'd just started up," Antoine objected.

Papa gave him a dark look, which Antoine could meet for just so long. Antoine turned away. "Where's my coat?" he asked.

I led him to it, right by the door where it always was. It was blue, with brass buttons, and it made him look quite respectable except for the shapeless felt cap he pulled from his pocket and put on his head.

"She was so beautiful," Antoine told me. "The last time I saw her, I was ten. I didn't remember her being so beautiful. I didn't realize how young she was."

I ignored his words. "I know what you need," I said, for the night air through the open window felt so cold. Almost a month too early, I brought out the woolen scarf I'd made to give Antoine for Christmas.

Antoine waited patiently while I placed the scarf just so around his neck.

"Be careful," I whispered to him.

"How many years have we been afraid of her?" he whispered back. "And what has she ever done?"

"Shh," I warned. If Maman heard talk like that, it would be the end of his errand for Jean-Pierre and his grandmother.

"Such a kind, sorrowful face," Antoine insisted. "Perhaps if just one person stopped to help her, maybe that would set her spirit to rest." Antoine's dark eyes were sad and concerned. Antoine always worried about other people, and of all the boys, he was the only one who had patience with Jean-Pierre.

But Papa had heard him, and Papa smacked him on the back of the head. In a whisper so that Maman wouldn't hear and worry, he said, "You're helping enough people tonight. If she comes, you forget this foolishness. You fly like the wind."

"Like the wind," Antoine assured us all with his jaunty smile.

We opened the shutters and looked up and down the street. No sign of anyone between here and the corner to the right. No sign of anyone between here and where the street wound its way to the top of the hill to our left. That was the extent of the ghostly lady's realm: whatever had bound her to this earth, she never went beyond the crest of the hill or around the corner, a total distance of four blocks, with many of the buildings built so close they touched.

With tears in her eyes, Maman kissed Antoine's cheeks. Drier-eyed, Grandpère did the same. Papa shook Antoine's hand, and I heard him whisper, "No foolishness."

"Of course not," Antoine agreed.

I waved, and Gaetan, Mignon, and Honorée—up from their beds without any of us having noticed—chorused. "Good-bye, good luck," as Antoine raced confidently down the stairs.

"Still all clear," Grandpère shouted from the open kitchen window, and Antoine burst, out of the front door.

He ran out into the middle of the street, but then instead of heading immediately to the corner, he turned to wave to us.

"Go," Papa said, gesturing him away. "Go!"

Antoine threw his cap in the air and called out a loud "*Whoop!*" so that when he would brag to his friends the next day about leaving the house during the hours of darkness, they'd know he spoke the truth.

Papa clapped his hand to his forehead in exasperation.

But Antoine took only that one extra moment.

Then, his blue coat flapping, his new scarf trailing behind, he ran to the corner—in under thirty seconds, by Grandpère's pocket watch, just as he had promised—and he disappeared from view.

Maman was so overwrought with Antoine's exuberance, she sat down in the parlor, fanning herself, not even sending the younger ones back to bed. So we stayed in the kitchen with

Papa and Grandpère. Anxiously we stared out the window and waited.

Within a half hour, there was a flurry of movement at the corner, and suddenly Antoine was back. With one hand he held on to his cap, because now he was running into the wind. He had his other hand in his coat pocket, by which we knew that he had succeeded in getting a new bottle of medicine from the doctor.

"Thank God," Papa said.

But a moment later he groaned.

I followed the direction of his gaze.

The ghostly lady was making her way down the hill toward us.

"Antoine!" Papa shouted.

Ten houses away, Antoine slowed down. Obviously he didn't hear. He took his hand down from his cap to press against his side. He must have run all the way back from the doctor's home, and now—when he most needed speed—he was winded.

Being higher up, we could see the ghostly lady was fast approaching, but Antoine could not.

"Antoine!" Grandpère and I and the children added our voices to Papa's.

Maman heard all our noise and she came rushing into the kitchen. She added her voice to ours, and Antoine's head swiveled in our direction. He stopped entirely. He grinned—I could see the flash of his teeth in the moon-light—and he held up the bottle for us to see.

"Run!" we shouted.

He tipped his head quizzically and pointed to his ear, indicating he couldn't hear. He probably thought we were cheering.

We pointed frantically in the direction of the hill.

From where he stood, I don't think he could see her yet, but he finally realized what we were saying. Continuing to our house was closer than going back to the safety of the corner. He jammed the bottle of Jean-Pierre's medicine into his pocket and took off at a run, so that his cap flew off his head and landed unheeded on the cobblestones behind him.

The lady was moving at an impossibly fast speed.

Other shutters were open, other people were shouting, "Run!"

The lady had reached the part of the street that leveled off, three houses to our left. Antoine was three houses to our right. But she was moving much faster than he.

Antoine was two houses away when she reached our building.

—when she stopped directly in front of our door.

—when she stood, her arms extended, blocking the way in.

Antoine stopped also, with no way to get around her.

Grandpère shouted, "Don't look at her eyes, boy!"

Then the ghostly lady took a step toward Antoine.

Antoine backed away.

But the lady's steps seemed to take her twice as far as Antoine's, and the distance between them was quickly disappearing.

The door to the hat shop across the street from the butcher flew open. "Antoine, here!" called Mademoiselle Cosette, who owned the shop.

The ghostly lady practically flew at the door, and Mademoiselle Cosette slammed it shut just in time.

This gave Antoine the chance to race ahead several meters, but in another moment the lady had caught up with him.

"Your eyes!" several neighbors shouted down.

Antoine raised his arm to cover his eyes.

The ghostly lady stood in front of him, but every time she tried to pull his arms down, her hands would pass right through him.

I stayed at the window just long enough to make sure that Antoine seemed safe as long as he wasn't looking at her. Cosette had given me an idea. If I could open our door for Antoine, that would save him several seconds and might be enough to make a difference. I raced down the stairs and cracked open our front door.

Antoine was still standing on the street, frustratingly close, his arms covering his eyes.

The ghostly lady was still ineffectively trying to get his eyes uncovered. But she was obviously confused, or distracted, by all the open shutters, all the doors open a crack, all the people—besides Antoine—within easy reach.

Across the way and down a shop and a half, Cosette saw me peeking out our door. She'd always liked my brother, though she was several years older. Now she called out, "Antoine! Can you walk with your eyes closed? Can you follow the sounds of our voices?"

Angrily, the ghostly lady rushed at her a second time.

At which point I screamed, "Antoine! Home!"

Cosette's door slammed yet again, and the lady spun around as Antoine leapt up the three steps separating our door from the street.

If there had been one step instead of three, he might have made it.

As it was, the lady stepped into the doorway, between the two of us.

I raised my hands to cover my eyes, but after a moment I peeked, for I had the impression that she was facing Antoine, not me.

I was right.

Antoine had his hands up, too. The lady had her hands resting, more or less, on his, though I could see she wasn't solid: her dress, constantly billowing, passed through my legs and Antoine's; her long, unbound hair streamed about her and I felt nothing where it passed through my arms.

There was no way she could harm us.

Then, so soft I tried to believe I hadn't really heard her, she spoke, for the first time in memory.

She said: "Please."

Antoine, who was kind even to simpleminded Jean-Pierre, slowly lowered his hands. I could see his face, not hers. But, through my fingers, I could tell he was looking directly into her eyes. He held out his hand to her, and this time her fingers clasped solidly about his. And then he became as transparent as she, and then they both disappeared.

There's a street in the village where I grew up that everyone knows not to travel down past sunset.

But we don't live there anymore, for my mother finally got her wish, and my father moved the family to the town across the river.

It was bad enough dealing with a sad, pale lady. But none of us could bear the thought of the ghost who had replaced her, with his sad brown eyes and the brass buttons of his coat twinkling in the moonlight as his woolen scarf billows in the breeze, which isn't necessarily there.

ABOUT THE AUTHORS

AL SARRANTONIO has written everything from horror and mystery novels to science fiction and humor. His work includes the horror novels *The Boy with Penny Eyes* and *House Haunted*, the science fiction novel *Moonbane*, and the mystery novels *Cold Night* and *Summer Cool*. His short stories have appeared in magazines such as *Twilight Zone* and *Isaac Asimov's Science Fiction Magazine*. He lives in New York's Hudson Valley with his wife and two sons, and is currently at work on his next novel.

PATRICK BONE is a retired parole officer who has worked as a ranch hand, minister, deputy sheriff, Telluride deputy marshal, prison captain, and college teacher. He lives in Littleton, Colorado, where he is a storyteller and writes poetry, songs, and fiction for children and adults. His stories have appeared in *Bruce Coville's Book of Monsters* and *Book of Ghosts*. He is putting the finishing touches on a picture book/audio cassette of scary songs and stories for kids.

CHARLES DE LINT is a full-time writer and musician and is currently writer-in-residence at the Ottawa & Gloucester Public Libraries. His latest book is *The Ivory and the Horn*, a second collection of Newford stories. He currently resides in Canada.

MARY FRANCES ZAMBRENO has a doctorate in medieval languages and literature. She has published two fantasy novels for young readers: *A Plague of Sorcerers* and *Journeyman Wizard*, and one of her stories appeared in *Bruce Coville's Book of Ghosts*. She teaches college in the Chicago area.

DEBRA DOYLE and JAMES D. MACDONALD, a husband-and-wife writing team, have published nearly two dozen books. One of their stories appeared in *Bruce Coville's Book of Monsters*. Their most recent books include *Knight's Wyrd* (young adult fantasy), *Judgment Night* (young adult horror), and *The Gathering Flame* (adult science fiction). They live in New Hampshire with their four children.

About the Authors

JUDITH GOROG is the author of many collections of scary, weird, and sometimes funny short stories—among them *Please Do Not Touch; In a Messy, Messy Room;* and *Three Dreams and a Nightmare.* She has been called "the Stephen King–type mistress of bump-in-the-night scary stories for young readers." Her forthcoming collections are *Beware the Snooping Sitter and Other Tales for Tonight* and *In a Creepy, Creepy Place.*

SHERWOOD SMITH lives in California. She began making books out of paper towels when she was five—usually stories about flying children. She started writing about another world when she was eight and hasn't stopped since. She has stories in several anthologies, including *Bruce Coville's Book of Aliens,* and has published three fantasy novels for young readers: *Wren to the Rescue, Wren's Quest,* and *Wren's War.*

LOIS TILTON is the author of two novels featuring vampires, *Vampire Winter* and *Darkness on the Ice,* as well as books written in the science fiction universes of *Star Trek* and *Babylon 5.* She has also published more than four dozen fantasy and science fiction stories in magazines and anthologies.

PAULA MCCONNELL has two passions, children's literature and writing, and only recently decided to combine the two. Her professions have included teaching assistant, full-time mom, costume designer, and Tupperware lady. She now is the manager of a children's bookstore within a larger bookstore. She lives in Syracuse, New York, where she hunts down new material with her three sons and an iguana named Makeba.

GORDON VAN GELDER grew up in New Jersey and attended Princeton University. He now lives in New York City, where he edits mystery and science fiction novels for St. Martin's Press. His short stories have appeared in *Young Blood, 100 Great Fantasy Short-Short Stories, Christmas Magic,* and elsewhere. His apartment tends to be messy.

S. ANTHONY GARDNER lives in a rural area a half-hour north of Syracuse, New York. He lives in a big house, on a small hill, across the road from a Scout camp and cemetery. He serves lots of spirits at his Halloween parties, and a few live people, too. He is happily married to a psychologist, and they have two cats who keep them busy. When he isn't writing, he works as a marketing and computer telecommunications consultant—which is a fancy way of saying he earns a living by writing and talking about writing.

VIVIAN VANDE VELDE lives in Rochester, New York. She shares her house with her husband, her daughter, a cat, a rabbit, and a hamster. She reports that her story for this book was inspired by the face of the ghostly lady a friend draped over her door one Halloween. She also wrote a story that appeared in *Bruce Coville's Book of Ghosts*. She has published seven fantasy books, the most recent of which are *Companions of the Night* and *Tales from the Brothers Grimm and the Sisters Weird*.

JOHN PIERARD, illustrator, lives with his dogs in a dark house at the northernmost tip of Manhattan. *Bruce Coville's Book of Spine Tinglers* is the fifth anthology he has illustrated in this series. His pictures can also be found in three of the books in the *My Teacher Is an Alien* quartet, in the popular *My Babysitter Is a Vampire* series, in the *Time Machine* books, and in *Isaac Asimov's Science Fiction Magazine*.

Photo: Jules

BRUCE COVILLE was born and raised in a rural area of central New York, where he spent his youth dodging cows and chores. Like most kids, he loved scary stories, and some of his fondest boyhood memories are of listening to—and later telling—tales of terror around a campfire. He now lives in Syracuse, New York, with his wife, illustrator Katherine Coville. Living with them are their youngest child, Adam, three cats (Spike, Thunder, and Ozma), and a dog named Booger.

Though Bruce has been a teacher, a toymaker, and a gravedigger, he prefers writing. His nearly four dozen books for young readers include the best-selling *My Teacher Is an Alien* quartet, as well as *Goblins in the Castle, The Dragonslayers,* and *Into the Land of the Unicorns.*

APPLE®PAPERBACKS

Pick an Apple and Polish Off Some Great Reading!

BEST-SELLING APPLE TITLES

- ☐ MT43944-8 **Afternoon of the Elves** Janet Taylor Lisle $2.99
- ☐ MT41624-3 **The Captive** Joyce Hansen $3.50
- ☐ MT43266-4 **Circle of Gold** Candy Dawson Boyd $3.50
- ☐ MT44064-0 **Class President** Johanna Hurwitz $2.75
- ☐ MT45436-6 **Cousins** Virginia Hamilton $2.95
- ☐ MT43130-7 **The Forgotten Door** Alexander Key $2.95
- ☐ MT44569-3 **Freedom Crossing** Margaret Goff Clark $2.95
- ☐ MT44036-5 **George Washington's Socks**
  Elvira Woodruff $2.95
- ☐ MT41708-8 **The Secret of NIMH** Robert C. O'Brien $2.75
- ☐ MT42537-4 **Snow Treasure** Marie McSwigan $2.95
- ☐ MT46921-5 **Steal Away** Jennifer Armstrong $3.50

Available wherever you buy books, or use this order form.

- -

SCHOLASTIC INC.
Box 7502, 2931 East McCarty Street, Jefferson City, MO 65102

Please send me the books I have checked above. I am enclosing $ _____ (please add $2.00 to cover shipping and handling). Send check or money order—no cash or C.O.D.s please.

Name_____Birth Date_____

Address_____

City_____State/Zip_____

Please allow four to six weeks for delivery. Offer good in the U.S.A. only. Sorry, mail orders are not available to residents of Canada. Prices subject to change.